CW00961615

CHRISTIAN
CRIMINALS

CHRISTIAN CRIMINALS

Chris Shimboff

To order additional copies of this book, contact:
Xlibris
1-888-795-4274
www.Xlibris.com
Orders@Xlibris.com
815590

CHAPTER 1

I GET UP OUT of bed and walk to the window. I pull back the shades and feel the sun on my face. I just stand there and soak it all in. Nice days seem to be so few and far between. I just know this is going to be a great day. We always go to church on Sunday and really look forward to it. We have Wednesday night Bible study too, and those are great, but I love my Sundays.

I start to put my suit on, and I can hear in another room as Jacob and Jessica are getting ready. Jacob is my son, who is now approaching ten years old, and Jessica is my fourteen-year-old daughter. My name is John Burton, and I am a middle-aged man who loves the Lord. I have been a software developer for the last twenty years, and I definitely know what I'm doing. I am also responsible for being the lead developer on many national projects.

Enough about me though. I know where my wife is. You probably can't smell it, but I sure can. Her name is Layna, and she is where she usually is, down in the kitchen, making yet another fine cuisine breakfast among other things. She loves the Food Channel, and quite frankly, I do too. In fact, I have a little bit of a belly to prove it.

I get down the stairs and quickly grab up my coffee mug and push it up to my nose. "Ahhh, yes, the smell of coffee in the morning," I remark. I begin to slowly sip my coffee. To me, nothing is as good in the morning as a nice hot cup of coffee. As we all sit down at the table to eat, we all bow and ask God to bless the food. We always pray, especially before we eat. I guess it might be obvious by now that we are Christians, but if it isn't, just hang with me, and you'll see.

We set out on the four-mile drive to church and hear some disturbing information on the radio. Now before I tell you what I hear, let me just tell you a few things. We have heard on the radio and television for the past two weeks threats of the government banning certain religions in America. That means no more congregating, socializing in a certain religious group, etc. The government feared that religion has too great an impact on the America that we live in today. Too many people do things in the name of religion and aren't afraid to die by it. Since our country has started doing this, there are also several other countries that were once free to religion that are now the same way. Canada and Mexico have both made the same type of declaration that America has made.

When all this information came to light, I assumed it would be these extremist groups or the really violent religions. I don't really know a lot about those other religions, but I know enough to know that they aren't Christian. Now the information that I heard on the radio was that several cities went into lockdown as a result of law enforcement agencies going in and closing down certain buildings with religious affiliation. As a result, they have had rioting and looting. I believe it to be some synagogues, mosques, and I even heard about a few covens being shut down.

I just know this has nothing to do with Christianity because this nation was founded on Christianity, and Christians are usually a very peaceful bunch of people. I assume they are doing all this to get this nation back where it was fifty years ago, when everybody respected God and valued morals.

We pull into the church parking lot and walk inside. As usual, we are greeted by an entourage of people. I believe we have an awesome congregation, and I believe we have the friendliest church you will ever know. We go into the sanctuary and sit in our normal seats and just wait for church to start. I just sit there and close my eyes and bask in God's presence. As the music starts, we stand and begin to sing. The words fill the air, and it just seems like God is especially pleased with us today as we can feel the Holy Spirit moving among us. As the music ends, we sit and prepare ourselves for the message that the pastor is going to preach.

As he gets about five minutes into the message, we hear the sirens outside go off. I look at my wife, and I can see the puzzled look on her face, and I'm sure I am sporting the same expression. I know it isn't a test because that was a week ago. The skies were crystal clear when we walked in. I keep trying to think to myself what is going on. I just dismiss it as human error and just continue listening to the message.

About that time, we hear the front doors of the church shatter and a loud commotion going on in the foyer. Being involved as an elder in the church, I get up to see what's wrong. About as quickly as I get up from the pew, military personnel come barging into the sanctuary and surround us. I feel like a dangerous criminal with the way they barge in and surround us. It is such an uneasy feeling having that many guns trained on me and my family.

A man casually walks into the sanctuary. He looks very dapper and professional. He reaches his hand into his jacket to get something out. What he pulls out is a piece of paper he has folded. When he pulls it out, he begins to read it. This is how it reads:

> *Effective this day, April 22, 2023, the new Law states that any affiliation with religion or religious activity is strictly forbidden and those who affiliate are committing a crime which is punishable by death. All buildings associated with religion or religious activity will be closed down effective immediately. Any person/persons who open up a building for any religious purpose will be put to death. Any person/persons caught with material for the purpose of learning, teaching or distributing of religion is a crime punishable by death. A grace period of approximately 24 hours will be granted for every individual to dispose of religious effects, at which time effective April 24, 2023, the law concerning any material found on a person or at a person's residence will go into full effect. This law has been signed by our lawmakers and passed by the Congress of the United States.*

He finishes and looks at us and says, "Since this law just went into effect, all of you who are here will be dismissed and will not be tried for being in a church, if you leave now with no resistance. Those of you who resist will be immediately executed as is instructed to us."

As he finishes up, my heart sinks down into my stomach. I think to myself and try to figure out how something like this can happen. This isn't supposed to be like this. My family slowly walks by them, a little unsure whether they can be trusted. As we make it out into the parking lot, I'm starting to feel as though we are getting a little closer to safety. I know what he says, but there is just something about that guy that can't be trusted. How can they do this? We have laws in place and amendments that protect American people. What has happened to our country?

We get into our car and slowly drive away. As we are driving away, we can see them preparing to put yellow police line tape on the doors to the church. I sit there in my seat, tears running down my cheeks. I am so overrun with sadness I don't know what to do but pray. I look over at my wife, and she looks at me, and she wipes a tear from her cheek. I look in my rearview mirror, and I can see both my kids crying as quietly as possible. This is no doubt a traumatic event, but what can we do? I love my family too much to have done or said anything in the sanctuary. As I sit and think about it, I think that maybe I should have said something. What would be the benefit of me getting blown away today? I'm so frustrated because I feel like I should have done something. My wife looks at me and said, "What are we going to do?" I reply quietly, "I don't know, but whatever we do needs to be God's will. We need to pray and find out exactly what that is."

As I drive home, I can see other churches in my community getting the same speech. The town looks like a military zone it's just crazy. I have never seen so many soldiers in one place like this. It truly looks as though we are going to war. War with whom? Is this to be another civil war, brother fighting against brother? I guess I'm just thinking all these different things and at the same time bouncing these questions off my Father in heaven. I'm looking for some clue as to what happened. The only think that I can even think could be is we have pushed God out of so much over the years. We pushed Him out of our schools, public places, government buildings, and at times, even our churches. I suppose this is what God is trying to tell me. We have brought this on ourselves. Why should my family have to suffer for the actions and ideas of the unrighteous? Quickly, the Holy Spirit tells me that it rains on the just and the unjust. I realize at this particular time, we need to ready ourselves for the fight of our lives.

We arrive at the house, and we all slowly make our way inside. As soon as I walk inside, I walk straight to my study. I walk in and drop down to my knees and start praying intently. "God, I don't know why this happened. Even though this has happened, Your Bible tells us that You will never leave us nor forsake us. So I have to believe that You are right here with me, Father. I pray that You will give me understanding and wisdom to know what I need to do in this terrible time. I ask, Father, that You keep my family and me safe from harm and that You meet our needs. Continue using us, Father, to bring people into safety, not so much physical safety, Father, but spiritual safety. We need Your Spirit now more than ever, Father. Amen." I know God heard that, and I know that He will take care of my family. I know that God's ways aren't our ways, but I just don't understand it. I had a pastor friend tell me once that God lets us do what we want (freedom of choice), and this is a result of our nation making many bad choices. As time progressed, rioting and looting seemed to flood the news as millions of people were protesting.

We are supposed to get rid of all our "religious" stuff, but I can't bring myself to do it. My Bibles, crosses, tapes, and CDs are among just some of many things I am supposed to get rid of. These items are really precious to me, especially my Bible. A Christian and their Bible are supposed to be like a bee is to honey. You should always have your Bible. I have to believe that God will win overall, and ultimately, if we lose our lives, we haven't necessarily lost. The Bible tells us in Matthew 16:25, "For whoever wishes to save his life shall lose it; but whoever loses his life for My sake shall find it." If you believe that, you have to believe everything else in the Bible because it is all authored by God. As I continue speaking to myself and letting the Holy Spirit minister to me, I realize this is where it all starts. There is a very distinct possibility that we won't survive this if we continue living this way. I'm not going to stop; I absolutely refuse to.

I make my way back out of my study and find a peace that only God can give me. I wish my wife and kids have the same peace. I walk up behind my wife as she is doing dishes and hug her neck. I say to her, "Don't worry, honey, God loves us, and He isn't going to let us fight this all by ourselves."

She turns and looks at me with tears in her eyes, and she says, "I know. I guess it is still just all sinking in and is very overwhelming. Our whole lives are going to be different now."

I know what she's talking about; this all seems so surreal. As I pause to keep myself from breaking down, I tell her, "Listen, we won't be able to go back to the building, but the church is right here in our hearts. Just like Paul and Silas in prison, they weren't happy to be there, but nobody, not even Satan, could take away their joy. Don't let Satan rob you of your joy. You may not be happy in your life at this particular moment, but because God's spirit still lives inside us, we have got to be full of joy." She sniffs and smiles, and I can see that it means something to her. "I'm going to go check on the kids and see how they're doing," I tell Layna in a whisper.

I enter Jacob's room and call to Jessica. She enters the room crying, and I look over at Jacob, and he is doing the same thing. It breaks my heart to see my kids crying. My eyes start watering, and I look at the two of them and say, "Listen, I love you guys very much! What happened is awful, and I don't expect you guys to turn your hearts to stone. Let me tell you, though, we have each other. I told your mom, and I am going to tell you the same thing, God is here in our hearts. I know you are going to miss going to church, but you will still be able to see your friends at school."

Jessica looks at me and mutters, "Most of my friends go to a different school, but why would those people close down our church? We didn't do anything wrong."

"I don't really have an answer for you, honey, but what I do know is this, this country has been shutting God out now for the last forty years. Take Him out of the workplace, out of the school system, out of the government system, and eventually, you don't have him anywhere anymore. I truly believe that since we as a nation have told God to get out of our lives, I believe that is exactly what He is doing, and when He leaves, so does His hand of protection. Now I don't know if that's the right answer, but I believe that it is."

As Jacob wipes his face, he looks up at me and says, "I think you're right, Dad, we aren't even allowed to talk about Jesus or bring a Bible to school anymore."

I tell them with confidence, "Just pray and believe that God is still right here with us. He is in control one way or another. If you truly believe that, you can't go wrong, no matter how bad things get or what they do to us." I stand and kiss both of them on the forehead and tell them everything is going to be all right, and then I walk out.

I sit with Layna and say to her, "Outwardly, I think some things should change. Like, for example, I should probably pull the bumper stickers off my car and should pull the fish off the back of the van. But inwardly, we don't have to change. In fact, I suggest that we keep everything in the house and just not invite anybody over unless we know them. We keep our Bibles and stuff safe inside."

A skeptical Layna looks at me and says, "Are you sure we should do that? You know what the guy said. If we get caught with any of this stuff, we will be put to death."

"That's why we keep all this stuff inside, no exceptions. Then they won't catch us with it." She nodded yes, but I can tell that she is nervous about it. I know she isn't afraid so much to die for the cause as she is scared for the life of our kids. I am also afraid for their lives, but we have got to make some kind of stand, and we as Christians need our Bible. "We need to continue going to work and paying the bills just like before this happened, and everything will be the same except Sunday. We just won't go to church. We will have church right there in our living room."

Layna replies, "Okay, I need that and so do the kids. We will do it."

I smile and gently touch her cheek and give her a kiss. My wife is so supportive, and she recognizes that we all need God time. The day progresses and night comes, and I get down on my knees by my bed and open my heart to God. "God, You know my heart and how I am feeling at this very moment. We will remain faithful to You, Father, no matter what. Just like Job, we will be steadfast and place our trust solely in You, Father. Please let me know Your will and direct me to do so. Thank You for hearing my prayer, and forgive me, Father, for where I have failed you, and thank You, Father, for never failing me. Amen."

CHAPTER 2

TWO DAYS LATER, and today is the day. This is the day that the law goes into full effect. I know God is going to take care of us, no matter what comes up. It is a fairly normal morning. Everybody is adjusting in their own way, but overall, everybody is doing okay. I give my wife a kiss and hug the kids and head out the door to work. I walk in the employee entrance to my job and make my way to my office. Of course, this stuff happened two days ago, and still, the halls are filled with discussion, gossip, and speculation about all that has happened or will happen.

As most of the day drags on, Glenn wanders into my office and casually closes the door behind him and sits. I give him a puzzled look and ask him, "Good morning, Glenn. What's going on?"

Now Glenn used to go to my church until it was closed, and we haven't had much discussion with anybody at the church about what happened. I guess everybody is still shook up. Glenn looks at me and says secretly, "What are you going to do about what's going on?"

I said what I guess anybody would say, "I am just going on about my life as if nothing happened. Should I be doing something?"

I trust Glenn, so I'm not opposed to telling him how I am feeling or, just simply put, the truth. Glenn whispers, "Did you guys actually get rid of your Bibles and stuff?"

I remarked with defiance, "Not a chance! We aren't going to change our homelife. They have changed our social life, but we refuse to change our homelife."

Glenn smiles at me and says, "We didn't change our homelife either." He smiles and then walks out.

I go on with my day as usual. For the most part, it has just been business as usual. If not for what happened at church on Sunday, I wouldn't have really guessed there was too much going on where I'm from. I know there is still rioting going on, but I can't imagine it hitting us in our small town.

I'm just noticing how the day is dragging on. I really want to get home to find out how my family is doing. I only have about another thirty minutes before I'm off and ready to go. I notice that everybody is making their way to the television we have in the break room. Interested to see if there are any new developments, I follow suit and make my way to the break room too. Before I can get to the television, I can hear some news station, and then I can hear the words "special news bulletin," and it goes something like this:

> *Everybody is aware of what occurred two days ago, and now we have a new development that has just been brought to light in the last hour. Law enforcement officials are now conducting an inspection of all residences, everywhere across the nation. Those who have "religious items" in their place of residence will receive the punishment of death set forth by the United States government. We are unclear at this point where the searches are going to begin to take place, but they have already started.*

Before the news reporter can say anymore, the news reporter stands and yells, "Hey, what are you doing? HEY, the people have a right to know!" The news reporter is pulled away from the camera, and then we hear the most terrifying sound I have ever heard, a gunshot. Then the camera goes off the air, and static is all that is left. I can't believe it. The news reporter was just killed on live television, and the network was just shut down. Oh my goodness! I cannot believe what is going on right here in my country. The land of the free is becoming something terrible. I look down at my watch, and it reads 4:30 p.m. Layna and the kids are already home. I need to get home and get them out of there. As I turn and look, Glenn is already gone, and I'm guessing he's headed home as well. Glenn actually lives on the same block as I do.

I run into my office and grab my things and dart out to my car. I speed out of the parking lot like there is no tomorrow. About a million things are running through my mind, and none of them are good. I can't seem to get home fast enough. As I'm driving home, I begin to say a prayer. "Father, please keep them safe until I get home. Make sure no harm comes to them before I can get them out."

I realize as I am saying this we are going to have to leave the house and never go back. We have too much stuff in the house to get out, and there is not enough time to hide it. I see the street I live on just a couple more blocks ahead. I begin to make the turn, and I see police cars everywhere and literally hundreds of military personnel entering houses and pulling families out of their homes. I see the police cars up ahead, and my heart sinks. I am trying to figure out what house they are at up ahead. I just know they are sitting at my house.

As I get closer to my house, I can see they haven't quite made it there yet. I can see that Glenn is standing on the lawn, talking to military people. As he is talking, I see that his family is being dragged outside by other officers. I see Glenn yelling and starting to charge the officers who are hurting his family. One of the officers hits Glenn with the butt of his rifle and knocks him down. I know what Glenn told me earlier, and he made it very clear that he still had all his stuff in the house.

I drive slowly, and I can see him, his wife, and daughter are put down on their knees like they are under arrest. As I was driving past, our eyes met as though to communicate. I can see fear in his eyes, and his wife and daughter are crying. I can see the worry and fear in his eyes, but I can also see the resolve in his face. At that moment, he has resolved to live for God, no matter the outcome. With no warning, three officers walk over to them and shoot all three of them in the back of the head. My mouth drops open in shock, and I begin to cry hysterically. Who does that to people? I have known Glenn for years, and they killed him with no remorse, with no second thought.

I pull into my driveway and see that my family is still home. As I begin to get out of my car, Janice, who is one of my neighbors, runs up to my car and whispers to me, "You have got to get out of here. Get your family and go. We will stall them as long as we can! We got rid of our stuff, so they won't find anything in our house. You guys take care."

As soon as I hear the urgency in her voice, my mind starts racing one hundred miles per hour. "OH NO!" I exclaim as I hurry up and run into the house. My mind is in full panic mode, but I have to keep cool so I don't look suspicious. I throw the door open and run around inside until I can find everybody. I gather everybody. "I thank You, Father, for keeping them safe," I mutter as I hug them. I look around at all the "contraband" in my house and know there is no way to hide it fast enough. As quickly as I can, I tell Layna to get the kids and get to the car as fast as she can move. I run into the bedroom and grab my money and my bankbooks as fast I can go. I jump in the car, where my family is already waiting for me.

Layna looks at me and asks, "What in the world is going on? I thought I was hearing gunshots."

I look at Layna with tears running down my cheeks. "They're all dead! I just watched Glenn and his family gunned down for having that stuff in their house. We're next!" Layna opens her mouth in awe and can't believe the words that I'm saying. I can see that she is surprised and very concerned about what is going on. There isn't anything we can do about it.

As I look in my rearview mirror, I can see the police approaching my neighbor's house and can see my neighbors standing outside. As my hands are shaking on the steering wheel, I turn to look at Layna and ask her, "They're doing surprise inspections of everybody's house. Didn't you see the news?"

She looks at me and says, "No, I was doing the laundry."

On the way to the bank, I can see this going on all over town. I tell the kids to get their heads down and close their eyes to pray. Layna and I are watching people all over town getting shot. Some of them are being shot by the military and others shooting back at the military. Layna covers her mouth in shock, and I can hear her crying. What can you do in a time like this? We feel so utterly helpless, and there is no way out of this. I keep thinking any minute I'm going to wake up, and this will all just be a bad nightmare. I've had no such luck in that regard.

We pull in the bank drive-through, and I withdraw all the money that I have. It isn't much, but it is enough to get us by for a little while. After collecting our money, we decide to stop and get something to eat. Truthfully, I'm not hungry, and I don't think Layna is either. The kids seem to muster an appetite. It is much easier to think about a plan or wait for God's plan when our stomachs aren't growling, so I decide to eat a little something.

We stop at a restaurant, walk in, and sit down to eat. We order our food and sit there patiently waiting. One word is not uttered the entire time we are waiting. I'm sure we're all thinking about our own little things that we wish would happen or not happen. Our food arrives, and we join hands and begin to pray. With a flash of a thought, the Holy Spirit urges me to raise my head. As I look up, there are about five other families looking at me with their eyebrows raised in surprise. "Oh my," I say as we quickly start eating. Some habits die hard, but this is one habit I really don't want to give up. Fact of the matter is, I will not give it up. I will just have to be more careful where and when I do that. So many changes we have to make.

Here is our problem: the cops are looking for us now that they have found all that "religious" stuff in our house. I guess that makes us fugitives, but I don't intend on letting my family fall into their hands.

As we finish eating, I look at my wife and say, "You realize we can't go back to work. We are going to have to stay off the grid." She looks at me, and it looks as though she just realizes what I am saying is true. If we continue to go to work, the police will know exactly where to find us. Too many people around here know us and know where we might be, so we decide it will be best for us to leave the area and go somewhere else, possibly going to a bigger city, where it's easier to blend in and avoid being questioned. So I fill the vehicle up with gas and hit the interstate to head to where we thought God wants us to be.

About 110 miles into it, we just cross the state line into Indiana, and I am thinking about stopping for a bathroom break. I look up in my rearview mirror and see a police car approaching from behind at an accelerated rate. Their lights are on, and so I slow down to see if they will pass me. Of course, things are never that easy. I start to feel the beads of sweat forming on my forehead. I can feel my heart beat harder and faster as I know I am caught. The butterflies in my stomach are relentless as I slowly make my way over to the shoulder of the road. As I stop, I can hardly breathe. It is as though somebody is squeezing my chest. The kids are sleeping, but my wife looks at me with the same worried look in her eyes as I am sure she can see in mine. I look at Layna and quietly say, "Pray, honey. If this is it, I want it to be as quick and painless as possible."

The officer approaches my car, and I can feel myself shaking. I just know we are in for it. As I roll down my window, the officer says to me, "Do you know why I pulled you over?"

I reply, "Not really, Officer."

He looks at me and says, "Well, you were going a little bit fast back there, about seven miles over the speed limit." I can't believe it. I was speeding, really? I must not have been paying attention thinking about everything else and where we were going to go. The officer says, "Well, I am going to need your license and insurance card." As I hand him my stuff, my hand is shaking, and I think he can tell I am a little nervous. He pulls his sunglasses down a little bit and crunches his eyebrows down and asks, "Are you okay? You look a little pale." I tell him I'm fine. I just need to get some food in me.

That is true, I was actually getting pretty hungry, and I do tend to get a little hypoglycemic. He walks his way back to the police car, and I have never prayed so fast in all my life. I say, "Father, if this is Your will, then Your will be done. If this is not Your will, Father, I ask that You show me favor here right now with this police officer. I need You, Father, right now. Thank You Father, for, hearing my prayer."

About that time, the officer walks up to the car and hands me my cards and says, "Sir, I am going to need you to step out of the car." Oh my goodness, I can't believe this. He's going to shoot me! I can feel my eyes welling as I know my wife has to watch me die, and my kids aren't going to know what happened to their dad. This must truly be the will of God. I step out of the vehicle, and he says to me, "Why don't you step back here?" I pace behind him slowly until we get back behind my vehicle, and he says, "What do you see wrong with this picture?" I stand there for what seems like twenty minutes, trying to figure out what it is he is talking about. He says, "I will give you a hint. Take a look at your back window." As he mentions that, my eyes train on exactly what he is talking about. I feel like I am in a dream. Kind of like when you are watching a movie and the camera is moving away from the object but getting closer at the same time. That is about how I feel at this particular moment. He looks at me and says, "Are you supposed to have a fish on your car that has Jesus in the middle?"

I look at him and shake my head. "I'm sorry, Officer, I thought my wife had taken care of this."

The officer replies, "I am going to let you go, but you need to get that taken care of, okay?"

I look at him and say, "I sure will, right now."

As I walk back up to the car, the officer says to me as he gets into his car, "Hey, God bless you!"

I walk back up to the car, and I know I look like I was just standing under a waterfall. I am completely drenched, and I look at Layna and say, "God came through for us again, and I doubted Him again. Forgive me, Father, for doubting You again. Thank You for keeping us safe yet again." I tell Layna that we have forgotten to take the window cling out of the back window. She gasps, and I tell her, "It's okay. Apparently, he was a Christian too, and he showed us mercy." I can see her beginning to pray and praise God.

It has been such a long day, and I am so tired. Everybody in the car is sleeping, so I decide now will be a good time to pull in and get a motel room. I pull in and see a motel that looks moderate. It isn't a dump, but it isn't a five-star motel either. I walk inside and tell the desk clerk that I need a room with two beds, and he says, "Okay, sir, it will just be a couple minutes while I get this set up."

As I wait, I turn around and watch the television, and about that time, a reporter comes on and says, "This is the list of people from the area who are missing and considered on the run. They are considered dangerous and a national threat." I see a list that is scrolling up on the television, and I see my name, along with Layna's, Jacob's, and Jessica's. That is so funny. Why would they think I am dangerous, let alone a national threat? Probably because I am breaking the law, and they consider willful, deliberate lawbreaking dangerous. Who knows? This country is falling apart anyway. Does anything make sense anymore?

"SIR!" the desk clerk says loudly as I jump out of my skin. He says, "I'm sorry, sir, I kept saying your name, but it didn't seem like you heard me."

"It's OK. I am just tired," I say in a weary and drained voice. I walk out to the car, and everybody is still snoozing. I sit quietly and drive us to the door outside the room. I gently nudge Layna and ask her to wake the kids up while I take the bags inside. Everything still seems to be a dream, like none of this can really be happening. I wish I can go to bed and, in the morning, wake up and everything be like it used to be before the government changed our life.

We get into the room and quickly get bedded down. I lie there for a second but can't seem to get to sleep. So instead of just lying there, I decide to get up and kneel at the bed and pray. I pray, "Father, thank You for getting us through another day. I don't know what your plan is yet, but I wait patiently. We only have a few thousand dollars left, Father. Please reveal where You would have us to go. I don't think You want us to just roam around aimlessly. Bless my little family, Father." I begin to cry before my Father, and I say to Him through the tears, "I beg You, Father, let this be a dream. But if it isn't, I desperately ask that You keep my family safe. If that isn't Your will, Father, then please make our death quick. I love my family so much, and I love You, Father. Amen." I lie down, and as I lie there, I quickly get drowsy thinking about heaven and soon being there.

CHAPTER 3

I T'S MORNING TIME already. Wow, I just fell asleep. I look around the room and see that I am the only one in the room. My stomach hits my throat, and my heart starts pounding out of my chest, and my breathing intensifies as I try to figure out where they can be. I call out, "Layna! Jacob! Jessica!" No answer. I jump out of bed and quickly run out to the motel sidewalk. I look around and see nothing but cars driving by and people walking on the street sidewalk. What in the world is going on? Where is my family? Of course, dozens of things start racing through my mind yet again. I close the door and go back in and sit on the bed. As I start to worry myself into an early heart attack, they walk in the motel door. I jump and yell, "Where have you guys been!"

Layna looks at me with a shocked look and says, "I'm sorry, we just thought we would let you sleep since you were up late driving last night. We just got some breakfast at the restaurant across the street."

I look at her with irritation and say, "Have you ever heard of notes!"

She replies with some attitude, "YES, but I thought we would be back before you got up."

"Whatever, as long as you are okay, but don't do that again! Let's go ahead and get our stuff packed up and get moving." I don't know where God wants us to go yet, but we need to stay on the move. I will continue driving us east.

I don't know why I am going east, but I feel like that is the direction we need to be going. I get onto the interstate and begin the day's journey to somewhere. I hear the kids in the back seat playing between themselves, and

Layna is reading some woman's book or something like that. I start meditating while I am driving and just start phasing the kids out. I phase the road noise out and the radio. As I pray for God's direction, it comes to me. "Aha!" I exclaim loudly.

Layna shutters as I startle her, and she says, "Good grief, what are you doing that for?"

I reply, "I know where God wants us to go!"

Layna's eyes become very large, and she says, "Well, are you going to tell me?"

I remark with delight, "He wants us to go to Philadelphia, Pennsylvania."

Everybody just sits there for a few minutes looking around at the expressions on everybody else's face. Layna says with a puzzled look about her, "We have never been there. How will we know where we are to go?"

"I don't know, but whatever God wants us to do, He will let us know."

As I continue on the road, I feel as though I have never had so much purpose as I do at this very moment. A person is so helpless when they don't know where they are going or what they are doing. We still have many miles left to go. Apparently, we crossed over into Ohio, and I didn't even know it.

The sun is beginning its descent into the horizon as we can start seeing the lights of Philadelphia. "Oh my goodness, this place is in total chaos," I say with some hesitation. "God, do You really want us here?" Of course, I don't get an answer, and the first thing that comes to my mind is Jonah. I submissively say, "Okay, Father, if this is where You want us, then this Nineveh is where we'll be."

We find a motel in the nonchaotic part of town and get inside. This place gives a very uneasy feeling as I can hear yelling and an occasional gunshot in the distance. I tell the family, "We aren't leaving this room tonight. I will just order us some pizza." The pizza arrives, and I give the pizza boy his money. We all sit down, and as we gather our hands together, I look around and smile at my family as we continue to practice what we believe to be important. We bow and say grace and ask God's blessing on the food. I tell you, pizza sure lightens the heart, but sure does bad things to the bowels!

We are all in bed now, but I feel as though God is trying to tell me something, and it is hard to hear when my mind won't slow down. I ask God, "Father, put my mind at ease so that I can hear what You are trying to tell me. I desperately want to know Your will for my family, Father. Thank You for keeping us safe thus far. Amen."

I dream that night of war. I remember my family and me struggling to make things happen. I remember seeing this symbol in my dream. It looks like a cross, but instead, it uses an infinity symbol for the crossmember. I keep seeing that over and over. I remember getting captured in my dream, and I was overwhelmed with emotion.

Morning time arrives, and we sit down to discuss what we are to do. I suggest to the family, "Let us walk around town today and see if God leads us a certain way. That will save us money for gas and will possibly allow us to strike up a conversation with somebody who might be led of God." We all agree that it seems like a good idea. Don't think, though, that I'm not worried about the rioting and the general behavior in the city. I can see the skepticism in their eyes. I wonder if they can see it in mine. We make our way out the door and begin to walk around "the city of brotherly love." As we walk around, there is so much this town has seen in the last few days. So much rioting and looting, but it seems like there is still so much good left.

I notice a marking on some buildings. As I get closer, I realize that they are what I was seeing in my dream. Maybe I saw them before I dreamed last night, and I just didn't realize it. I tell Layna about my dream and explain to her what I am looking for. When we see the symbol, she looks at me in surprise and asks if this is the symbol in my dream. It is definitely what was in my dream. They catch my eye because they aren't everywhere, and they are small. I've noticed from different places that some of them are red, and some are white. It is very confusing but intriguing. Maybe it is a weird Philly gang that uses this symbol. Frankly, there is a lot about this town that I don't know. Layna suggests that God could have given me the insight so I would know what to look for. Well, I found it, now what?

With a day of what seems to be an absolute waste, I am exhausted. I know the kids are exhausted; we have been walking around town all day. As everybody gets ready for bed yet again, I look at Layna and say, "I am going to go for a little walk, and I will be back shortly." Layna's face changes from tired to concerned. I touch her on the cheek and tell her, "Don't worry, babe, God will take care of me. I believe there is something about those symbols that God wants me to know." I give her a kiss, and I walk out the door. I had been thinking about the symbols that I had seen all day. We really only saw a handful of them, but why were some of them red and some of them white? I don't know why or what I am even thinking by going to look at one up close, especially at night. I think if they are what I think they are, there might even be some Christians close by or, at the very least, something that God wants me to see. Now that the sun has gone down, that's when criminal mischief seems to take over. I have to believe, though, that God is ultimately in charge here and leading me where He would have me to go.

I am walking down the same street we were walking down earlier. I can't remember exactly where I saw that symbol, so I am being cautious not to miss it. There doesn't seem to be anybody in sight within miles. It seems to be a pretty quiet part of town. I see alleys and old buildings but no people.

As I look around, I notice a sound behind me. Of course, everything is a little eerie anyway. The hair on my arms start rising to the occasion, and it feels as though every hair on my head is standing straight. As I turn around to see what the noise was, I hear a police car chirp his sirens. I quickly turn back toward the police car. They pull over and get out their car. They both approach me, and the one cop says, "What are you doing out in this part of town at this time?" The other cop chips in by saying, "Yeah, somebody walking around this part of town at this time could get hurt." At this very moment, I'm thinking I would have had better luck with whatever I thought was behind me. The cop says, "Do you have some ID, sir?"

"Oh, of course, Officer," I reply as I reach for my wallet. With a puzzled look on my face, I say, "I must have left it at my motel room."

The cops smile at themselves and say, "Sure you did. Why don't you come with us, sir, and we will help you to remember who you are?" I know this isn't going to be pretty.

We arrive at the police station, and I know this isn't going to be good. The cops have already had a news bulletin out on many people, me included. I'm sure not going to point them in the direction of the motel and condemn my whole family to my fate. The sergeant comes to the cell and says to me, "Listen, if you cooperate with us, this will go a whole lot smoother and better for you."

I look at him with a disgusted look and say, "Why was I arrested! I did nothing wrong, and they had no grounds for arresting me."

While he was smirking, he says, "Well, you couldn't produce identification, which means you have something to hide, and the officers believe you are a wanted criminal."

I yell, "You have no proof of anything!"

The sergeant walks away with a smile on his face, and I get to sit there and wonder what's going to happen. At that particular moment, the Paul and Silas story really rang true. I start laughing because of the irony. I say, "God, You do move in mysterious ways. I am going to do exactly what Paul and Silas did in prison." As I convince myself that it is the right thing to do, I begin to sing.

As I finish up my song, the sergeant walks by and says, "I thought so. We have something special planned for you." I bet they do. They don't seem to know God or love for that matter.

What is my family going to do? They are never going to move on knowing they never found me. I begin to cry and realize I'm never going to see them again. I begin to mutter a prayer. "Father, I'm a little confused about why I'm here. Maybe I wasn't supposed to come here at all. Maybe that wasn't Your voice that I heard. I really felt like that was You telling me to be here. I'm sorry,

Father, for not listening more closely and putting myself in harm's way. I pray, Father, that You send a guardian angel to protect my family and convince them that I'm dead and to do whatever they need to do to stay alive. I give everything over to You, Father. I love You, and I'll see you soon. Amen." I lay my head down and slowly drift away.

CHAPTER 4

"WAKE UP! WAKE up!" says this still small voice. I slowly open my eyes and look around, but I'm alone. It was probably somebody in another cell. I slowly drift back off to sleep. "Wake up!" This time it was much louder. I get up and approach the bars and look around. I don't hear anybody or even see anybody. I say very quietly, "God, is that You?"

God replies, "Yes, you're never alone. It is time for you to go."

Oh great, now I'm hearing things. God is the one who "told" me to come here, and I'm in jail. I'm pretty sure I'm just hearing things. I mean, how many times have you been in a situation and all of a sudden, you think about scriptures that you've read? That's all this is, just me hearing things. Then I hear the same thing again. I have to tell you, this sure sounds legit. I figure I better play along, just in case it actually is God. I reply, "Father, I would go, but I'm in jail. I can't get out of here." I am actually laughing a little on the inside because it does sound a little condescending saying what I said.

Assertively, God replies, "All you have to do is open the jail door." I'm not one to argue with God, but they lock these doors for a reason, and nobody has been by to unlock it. I know I have that look on my face, you know, the one that says this is pointless. Besides, even if the door were to open, this place is full of cops. There is no way they are just going to let me leave. You know what, I'm dying anyway. What do I have to lose at this point in time?

So I just get up and go over to the door. Before I push on the door, I look up as if to say I told you so. I push on the door, and it opens up. I stand there for a minute to see if some kind of alarm goes off, but nothing happens. I take one step out of the cell to see if somebody comes running up to me and throw me back in, but nothing. I leave the cell and open this other heavy-duty door with what looks like big locks. Apparently, this door isn't locked either. As I make my way out, I notice that all the cops are doing everything that they seem to always do. I continue walking without anybody saying a word to me. Up ahead, I see the exit sign. I continue walking the same pace so as to not be noticed. As I walk out the front door to the police station, I am just completely overrun with emotions. How in the world did this happen? Why didn't they see me? I can't figure out how all this came about. I hear God say, "Son, I am with you always, even unto the end." As tears stream down my cheek, I look up and say to God, "Father, I love You! Thank You." It is God whom I have been hearing. That is His voice that I have been hearing. Maybe I am supposed to be here!

I wipe the tears from my eyes and wave down a taxi. The cabbie drops me off at the motel, and I walk to the door and quietly knock. I would just go in, but the cops still have my keycard and stuff. At least I still have my wallet in the motel room. My wife opens the door quietly so she doesn't wake the kids up. She looks at me with worry and says, "What happened? I have been so worried about you." I point to the taxi, and she goes and pays him. I begin to tell her the story about what happened. As I'm telling her the story, I can see the awe on her face. I still don't believe all of it myself, and I'm the one who experienced it.

It is a very late night, and even some would call early morning. I should be going to bed, and I should even be tired, but so much has happened I just can't sleep. God is showing Himself to me in a real and true way, and in some ways, it is extremely overwhelming. I lie there thinking about how truly magnificent our God really is, and that doesn't even touch the tip of what God really is. I can slowly feel myself drift away.

I have another dream. This dream has the same symbols as the night before. I remember seeing a white symbol, and something happened in my dream, but I can't really remember. I remember being threatened to be killed. In my dream, this guy puts a gun to the back of my head, and right before he pulls the trigger, I wake up.

I can feel the sunlight on my face and just soak it up. As quick as I can think, I sit up in bed and feel myself quickly panic. I realize I got out of jail last night. I'm not still there. Was that a bad dream? No, I was definitely there last night. No matter how many times I tell myself that, it just seems surreal. I can't name one person that I know who has that happened to. I sit up quick enough that I woke Layna up, and she, in turn, woke the kids up.

Jacob looks at me with a worry on his face and asks, "Dad, are you okay? We were really scared last night that something bad happened to you." Jacob begins telling me he had a bad dream last night that I was going to be shot, and it had something to do with those symbols we had been seeing. I feel like God had me there last night for a reason.

I sit Layna and the kids down, and I tell them what happened last night. I explain to them that I feel like I'm on to something and that stopping now would be a bad idea. God delivered me from jail for a reason, and I'm going to make sure I find out what that reason is for me and my family.

I exclaimed, "Let's go eat somewhere! I'm in the mood for pancakes!" I know for me, breakfast food always seems to lighten the spirit and makes me feel better. I think we all know that by me going out, there is always a good chance that they will see me again. We sit there, and as our food starts to arrive, it dawns on me. We don't have to bow and close our eyes to pray to God. I look around at my family and quietly say, "You know something, we can still pray!" They are looking at me a bit strangely, so I figure I had better elaborate. "God knows that we're thankful, and He also knows what we're going through right now. Why don't we simply not bow our heads and keep our eyes open and just say a prayer that way? This way, when somebody looks over here or walks by the table, they won't know what we're doing. It will look as though we're just talking to one another." Jacob smiles, almost like that little smirk I see when he's being a little defiant. Clearly, this is piquing his interest some. So we don't bow, and we continue to look at one another, and I say a little prayer. It makes me feel real good praying before eating.

The symbols are still creeping into my thoughts. What if I bounce some ideas off Layna and the kids? It might put my mind to rest as to what they could mean. "Layna, I have something to ask you," I said as I finished off my pancake. "We know we are here for a reason." I start talking to them about the symbols that we have been seeing all over town, and not only the symbols, but they were also colored red and white. Of course, Layna starts thinking about what it could be.

Knowing Jacob, he blurts out the first thing he can think of. "IT'S A CROSS!" We just sit there and think about it. Yes, it does sort of look like a cross, but why would they draw it like that?

"Ummm, that could be, Jacob, but let's keep thinking about it," I tell him while looking fairly puzzled. Several ideas pop up, and some of them seem like real viable options, but something inside me says no. I do keep coming back to the cross idea.

We finish up eating and head out back to the motel room. As much as we all have "cabin fever," we can't just be wandering around Philly aimlessly. We sit in the room watching television, reading the Bible, or whatever we can do to keep ourselves occupied. As soon as the sun goes down, I decide to go ahead and get going. I look at my family and tell them, "I love you, guys. Please pray for me as much as you can until I return home."

Layna looks at me and says, "You're not going out again tonight, are you? You almost got killed last night."

I remarked, "Yes, I am going. God has something for us, but I need to trust in Him. Besides, I didn't die, and God delivered me in a remarkable way. I'm not saying I'm invincible, but God isn't done with me yet."

Layna doesn't really say anything else except "Hey, when you get back, I would like to sit down and talk to you about something."

I nod in affirmation, and she gives me a hug and kisses me, and then I walk out the motel room door.

I start my trek to a few locations that I know have the symbols. I come across a white symbol, and then I start examining it. When I look at it, very simply put, it does look like a cross. However, I realize the infinity symbol means something to the cross. Maybe this symbol means something, so I look around for a trapdoor or maybe a secret passageway on the side of the building. My search yields no fruit, I'm afraid. Hmmm, maybe I need to try a different one. I start to walk away, and I hear a voice out of the shadow, "What business have you here?"

After feeling like I need to change my underpants, I respond, "I'm sorry, I was just looking for something and noticed that marking on the building. I didn't mean to bother you. I was just looking." I start to walk away, and a man walks out of the shadows in front of me. As I turn to go the other direction, I see a handful of men walk out of the shadows. In my best kung fu voice, I say, "Waaaaaaaaaaaaa . . . Hiyyyyaaaahhhhh!" I must look like an idiot standing here poised like Bruce Lee.

The guy in front of me says, "It's time for you to be following us!" I'm thinking, *I don't think so.* A guy behind me pulls out a gun and insists I follow him. Of course, I realize after seeing that gun I'm not the argumentative type anyway.

I follow them into a doorway that also has the symbol on it. As I walk through this doorway, I see many people down here, and they are looking at me. I think I'm in the sewer system somewhere. The guy behind me nudges me in the back and pushes me into this small room. There is nothing in this room but a small light. I see in front of me a couple of men. One of them was the man who was in front of me in the alley. I start to speak, and the guy behind me kicks the back of my legs, and I go down to my knees.

"If you ever want to see the light of day again, you better tell me what you were doing in my alley!"

Okay, at this point, I definitely need a new pair of shorts! "I was just looking around honestly. I meant no disrespect," I reply again.

I feel the point of the gun on the back of my head, and the guy pulls the hammer back. "I'm giving you one more chance to talk to me, and then I'm redecorating this room with your brains!" says the guy behind me.

"God sent me here! I've been looking for signs of what He would have me to do, and I was intrigued by the symbols. I thought maybe that is what God was wanting for me. I swear that's the truth!"

The guy in front of me stares at me with his best poker face. He then starts laughing, and the guy standing next to him is smiling. "God! God! You're here because of God?" the man asks.

"Yes, sir!" I reply.

"Okay, I'll tell you what. You don't look like a stupid guy. I will let you go but only if you denounce the name of God. You must denounce His name, and then I will let you go. If you don't denounce the name of God, I will finish what I started with this gun!"

Okay, so I'm thinking, I did get mixed up with people who are not only unsavory to say the least but also hate God. Great! I slowly bow and mutter a quick prayer, "This is it, Father, forgive me for anything that could be separating me from You. Take care of my family. I love You, Father. Amen. Okay, you can shoot me now. I won't denounce the name of God. I'm a Christian through and through, and nothing is changing that." He looks at me and then tells the guy behind me to pull the trigger. I close my eyes, and with tears rolling down my cheeks, I tilt my head back slightly.

I hear a click. I slowly open my eyes, and I see the guy in front of me with his hand open, offering to help me up. "You did well. I'm very proud to call you brother! My name is Bob Cranston," he says to me with a smile on his face.

I reply, "I don't get it. Why didn't you kill me?"

"We are all Christians down here, and we pretty much know everybody here, but those of you whom we don't know, we have done the same thing to. We wanted to make sure that you were hardcore Christian and that you wouldn't divulge this information if military personnel threatened your life." I can't believe it—other believers!

He goes on to explain that Philadelphia has been going through stuff similar to this for quite a while, well before it was even announced federally. So they have started ramping up what they are going to do, and an underground church seems to be the only option. He tells me that Christians have been persecuted, and others have been burning churches there for quite a while, so they instituted this underground network of churches that only believers know about. I ask him what the symbols are and how everybody meets. He tells me that the symbols are a code for the Christians. This is how the Christians know where God's people are meeting and when they are meeting. He asks me to come with him. As we all walk out, he shows me the door and tells me, "See, this symbol is how we know where the entrance is. The white symbol indicates an even day of the week, and a red symbol indicates an odd day of the week. We do meet seven days a week, but those symbols tell us where we're meeting. We have a number of people who are our 'generals' who have been assigned locations on those specified days. We always meet at 7:00 p.m., and you're always welcome to attend services at any of the locations having service. We just ask that you are very careful to look around and ensure you're not being followed. We don't need any more of our brothers or sisters killed because of carelessness."

I ask him what the symbol actually is. It looks like a cross but not really. He smiles and then says, "Sure, it is a cross, but we didn't want to make it look too much like a cross, so we added the infinity symbol as a reminder that God's love for us is infinite as He sent His son to the cross to die for us." That's pretty cool and creative.

So we continue talking, and he tells me if they ever feel threatened in a certain area, they will just simply erase the symbol since it is chalk, and that way, people won't know what's there. I ask him how many locations they have around town, and he tells me that they have upwards of one hundred locations around town. I can't believe what I'm hearing–they have quite a network! I'm so excited to tell the family. He tells me that they have people around town who are in positions of note that help when they can, and they provide food and other needs for those who cannot work since the military are looking for some. I tell him that I've already had a run-in with the police here. He says, "That's okay. Just try to get work if you can. If not, we have a place for you."

CHAPTER 5

I'M SO EXCITED to get back to the motel and tell my family all that has happened. I know they are going to be thrilled to hear that we have a church family already and a little protection in numbers, as it were. I start my walk back to the motel with a new family, and I couldn't be happier. I feel invincible, revived, rejuvenated; I just can't explain how happy I am at this moment. I don't feel alone anymore. I turn my last corner before the motel, and I see squad cars in the parking lot. As I take a closer look, I see it's our motel room. OH NO!

I see somebody standing close by, and I walk up and ask them as casually as I can, "What's going on? Do you know?"

"Yeah, a couple dangerous fugitives were found to be staying here. I hope they find the worthless criminals and slaughter them!" I wonder if he even knows why the police are chasing us and that we aren't dangerous.

I look around, and I don't see our vehicle. That's odd. I wonder if it was towed away or if they drove away. I feel so helpless! Where's my family! In a panic, I start making my way back down to where I met Bob. As I approach, I see the symbol gone. So I decide to look around and see if I can find another symbol. I see one about a block away from the original, but it's also white, which means it won't be for two more days.

Well, that's great. I know where they're meeting. I really need to get some contact information for some people in there. So once again, I feel helpless. My wife and my kids are probably somewhere in Philadelphia, probably looking for me, and I'm looking for them. I slide down the wall in this lonely alley and put my head down on my knees and begin to cry. "Father, I need Your help! I can't do this without them. Help me, Father, to see where they will be and what I need to do. I am desperate, Father. Please help me!" I prayed through the tears. I decide that just sitting there crying isn't going to bring my family back.

I go to the nearest phone booth and look up the number to the police station. I call the nonemergency number, and I ask the lady on the other end of the phone if a Layna Burton was arrested earlier today. She tells me that she is in the jail, and she is awaiting trial for suspicions of religious contraband. I ask her if bail has been set, and she tells me not until in the morning, when she stands before the judge. I hang up the phone and realize they are going to kill my wife! My kids are likely going to be killed too. I need to find them. I make my way back to the hotel room and picked the lock to get into the room. I gathered up what stuff I could find and put it in a box I found. I can't help my wife right now, at least not until morning. I call around and find out my kids are being held at the juvenile detention center. It's only about a mile away, so I start the walk.

As I'm walking down the street, I pray for Layna. "Father, touch Layna just now, in the name of Jesus! Comfort her, Father, and let her know that she isn't alone. You tell us this in Your Word, Father, so I pray that she claims it, and I know You honor it. I don't know if I'm allowed to, Father, but I ask that you let her know that I'm thinking about her and praying for her. Amen!"

I see the detention center just ahead, and I look up to heaven as if to say "It's up to You now, Father." I walk in the front door and walk up to the reception counter. "Yes, I'm here to transport Jacob and Jessica Burton to the facility. She looks at me, and I can see the confusion in her face. This lady looks like something from a horror movie, and trust me, she put the villain to shame! She starts nibbling on a wart she has just inside her mouth. How disgusting is that! I look at her and wink and say, "They are Christians, if you know what I mean."

She begins to nod in affirmation. "Ahh, yes, I know what facility you're talking about now. The one over on the west side of town." I just smile so as not to lie about where I'm taking them. She looks at me and says, "Okay, I will have them brought up. Do you have your state identification card on you?"

Oh my goodness, what in the world is she talking about? "You don't recognize me? I can't believe that! Okay, I'll see if I can find it here." I tell her with irritation as I start looking through my wallet.

"Well, now that you mention it, I think I do remember you! You know what, I'll take care of the number. Don't worry about it!" she exclaims.

I look at her and smile and give her a little wink. She giggles just a bit, and I'm feeling like I'm going to throw up all over her and the counter. God, please forgive me.

I see the kids coming through the doorway just before the exit, and I start thinking about what I'm going to say. As the kids clear the door, I say, "Let's go, you stinking brats. We have some place special for you." I turn and smile at the lady at the counter, and she smiles back as best as she can. It's almost like looking at a hippo smile back at me. She has a big mouth and only a few teeth.

We make our way outside, and I tell them quietly to just keep walking and don't say or do anything else. I notice there are a few cameras here and there, but I don't know which ones I don't see. We get where I think we are far enough, and I drop to my knees and squeeze them as hard as I can. It's so good to feel them in my arms again! I tell them, "I love you guys so much, and I'm so happy to have you back. We need to get out of here because it may not take them long to figure out that I don't work for the state of Pennsylvania, and we also need to figure out how to get your mom back."

As night just continues to get darker and darker, I start wondering where we are going to sleep for the night. All my money is pretty much gone, and the hotel is a bad idea. We are walking, and I can see my kids getting very tired. I start praying to myself, "Father, I thank You so much for bringing me my kids. I love them so much, Father, and I know You do too! I want to make a small request, Father. Will You please provide us a place to sleep tonight?" It wasn't too long after I pray I can see up ahead an abandoned building of some sort. I look at the kids, and I tell them that's where we are sleeping tonight. I know this isn't an idea they relish, but desperate times call for desperate measures.

We walk in what appears to be a doorway of some sort, could be where the wall fell apart. As I get inside, I can see that we aren't the only ones staying here. In fact, there are at least fifty people all over the place in here. We wade through the endless bodies lying around. I hear a "pssss." I look around, and I see a young woman sitting by a little campfire. She says, "I have some room here if you want to join me." I don't really see any reason why not. It looks as though space is at a premium in this building. I nod and smile at her, and we all sit by the fire.

Jessica looks up at me and asks, "Daddy, I'm getting really hungry. That food in that place back there wasn't very good." I caress her head and embrace her to comfort her. The lady who we're sitting by picks her pot by the fire and offers us some beans. Truthfully, beans never looked so good. I think it's been a long time since I had any food, or so it seems.

We didn't really have much to say to one another. I thank her very much for letting us sit with her. As we lie there, I start thinking about Layna and how empty I feel without her! I start going through my mind what is going to happen to her, and I start becoming overrun with emotions. I don't even want to live without my wife, and just the thought of losing her is just too much to bear. I can feel tears streaming down my face, and I fight the urge to cry out loud. As I lie there, I begin to feel the presence of the Holy Spirit and feel Him touch me to comfort me. I start to realize that Satan is giving me these ideas to wear me down and break my spirit. I'm going to trust God and trust that He knows what's going on because I certainly don't. I feel myself slowly dozing off.

All of a sudden, I wake up to people screaming and running. I look around and realize that the military are raiding the place and looking for specific people. I grab Jacob and Jessica and start running out the door. It looks like it's in the early hours of the morning. I can see the sun lighting up the eastern sky but can't see the sun yet. We run about two blocks, and then we hide in a dumpster. My goodness, there is just no rest at all it seems. I hear somebody approaching, and I hear them talking. "Yeah, I think they came this way." Oh no! They know we came this way. There isn't really that much down this alley for people to hide except this dumpster. I can hear them getting closer and closer to the dumpster. I look around in the dumpster as quietly as possible for something to defend myself. The only thing I can find is a banana peel. I shake my head and grab the peel. I rear back as if I have the very sling that David used against Goliath. The door comes open, and I chuck it with all I have. SLAP! It hits this guy right in the face! Wait! We are with Bob! We are Christians too!

"Oh my goodness! I am so sorry! I really didn't know who you were!" I told him as I'm sure my face was as red as can be.

"Well, from my point of view, you sure seem dangerous with a banana peel," he says as he smiles. I can't believe it. I hit a guy who's trying to help me. "Follow us," he says.

We get out of the dumpster and start following him. "Excuse me, sir, what are your names?"

He replies, "I am Dave, and this is Dan," as he pointed to his sidekick.

"It's a pleasure to meet you, guys. I'm John, and this is my son, Jacob, and my daughter, Jessica," I reply.

He smiles and then replies, "It's a pleasure to meet you, guys. Just keep up with us." I see Dan open a manhole, and they go down the hole. "Come on, guys, you need to get down here before you're seen!"

I lower Jessica and then Jacob down the hole. I slowly make my way down the hole and then pull the manhole back over the hole. I can't see a thing. One of the guys pulls out a flashlight. He shines it around, and oh boy, does it stink down here! Dave says, "You know, don't mind the smell. You will get used to it after a while." I'm thinking, *There is no way a person can get used to this*. I wish I can describe it to you, but it is just too disgusting to describe and too unique to figure out.

We continue down through the tunnels, and the smell gets worse. Dan says, "We know who you are. Bob told us to find you and look out for you as soon as you and he parted company. We were trying to find you and caught up with you at that building right before it was raided."

I reply, "That's great, I appreciate that, but where are we going?"

Dave shines the light at me and replies, "We are going to our main center. We make it smell like this using a variety of things we find. We figure if people smell it and it's disgusting, they won't mess with it. If Bob didn't trust you, he wouldn't have authorized us to bring you here."

We continue for a ways, and the little tunnel goes from a twelve-foot tunnel into an opening about the size of a football field. "Wow! What is this place?" I ask.

"This is where they used to work on waterlines, gas lines, et cetera before this part of town was deserted. Now this side of town just has a few people living in it. Nice thing is, it still has city water and city gas and all that stuff running through these lines. We have learned how to tap into them to use appliances for heating and running water and things like that. You can see there, those are vents that lead to outside. The exhaust that we burn off using the natural gas exits this area through those vents," Dan elaborates.

This place is absolutely amazing. They have a small town down here. I look around, and it almost looks like it's set up in pods. Like there are group leaders and fifteen or so people in each pod. They have electricity down here, and they are actually growing food down here using UV bulbs. I would imagine you could survive for months down here, so long as the water, electricity, and natural gas held up. Dave and Dan take us to this small office-looking area, and low and behold, there is Bob!

"I suppose you're wondering why I didn't bring you down here to begin with," Bob asks.

I reply, "Well, it did cross my mind."

"You see, we have about four hundred people down here. At this point, we have room still but running out of room. We only have two options, expand the room out or stop growing. Some of our people live up top just fine with no problems, so they don't need to be here," Bob explains.

"I understand what you're saying and why you didn't tell me. I guess I should have told you that I have a warrant for my arrest. In fact, my wife and I both have," I explain to him. As I stand there, I can feel the tears welling up in my eyes. My mind starts drifting to thoughts of Layna. Bob looks at me and asks me what's wrong. I start telling him what had happened and that my wife was arrested and that she will be going before the judge in the morning for warrants on religious contraband.

Bob looks at me and definitely shows concern. He says to me, "Okay, let me work on this, and I will see what we can come up with, okay? In the meantime, you guys go see your squad leader. Her name is Mary, and she is very nice and very efficient. I think you guys will get along nicely." He looks at Dan and tells him to go ahead and take me over to meet Mary.

As we walk, we can see people looking at us, and they smile at us as to welcome us. We get over to where Mary is standing, and she introduces herself. "Hi, my name is Mary. I have been down here for a good while. I have been a squad leader now for about three weeks and really enjoy helping out. Each of our pods is broken up into families. You guys will be here. You have a bunk bed and a queen-size bed. You guys will have to share a dresser though. We have a shortage of those right now. Over here is our kitchen area. Everybody in this pod shares the kitchen. You see that door over there? Those are the community bathrooms. We all have to share those. Do you have any questions?" I shake my head no and thank her for the tour and helping us out. She smiles at me and mentions that if we need a shower, those are available right around the corner from the bathrooms. I think showers sound good. So we go ahead and get settled in to our area, although we don't have anything to put into the dressers.

We get done taking our showers, and another lady walks over from another pod. She brings us a couple of bags of clothes. She says, "I think these things will fit you and your family. It isn't much, but it should provide you with a couple changes of clothes." I couldn't thank her enough. These clothes that I'm wearing have been on me long enough to find their own way to the dirty clothes hamper. She walks back to her area. It's still in the very early hours of the morning, and I'm still very tired. I tell Jacob and Jessica to go ahead and lie down too. It's kind of weird sleeping in a big room with no walls, but we're tired enough to make it happen.

As I lie there, I begin to say a little prayer. "Father, I'm so tired and weary. I desperately need Your help. I feel as though I have been walking the path and doing Your will, but I'm just exhausted. I pray, Father, that You provide me with the strength I need to figure things out tomorrow and that You give us a way to get Layna out of the hands of the enemy. I lay this at Your feet, Father, and I thank You for so many answered prayers thus far! Amen."

I slowly drift off to sleep thinking about what is coming tomorrow and about Layna and days when we were happy and things were good. I think about the intimate moments we shared together and the fact that sleeping in an empty bed without her is one of the worst feelings I have ever known.

CHAPTER 6

$\mathbf{B}$OB COMES AND sits on my bed and gently shakes me to wake me up. "Listen, your wife is going to be going before the judge here in a couple hours. There isn't a whole lot I can do for you besides just praying for you and your family," Bob says quietly.

I respond with panic, "I thought you guys had pull up top? How come you can't do anything about this?"

He replies, "John, listen, I have some pull up top, but if I was that powerful, we wouldn't be hiding down here. I'm sorry, I wish there was more that I could do. We do have an attorney that is going to represent her, but they have been very hard on people with convictions in this arena. Be ready in about forty-five minutes. We will be going to the top to see the outcome of the court. You can leave your kids here. They will be safe and well cared for."

I lower my head and worry about what's going to happen. I begin to cry. I feel so emotionally ran down. I feel sad and pain in every part of my body. I don't know what else to do besides just pray. I start praying. "Father, I have never been closer to just giving up. I am so tired in every part of my body. My time here has been a roller-coaster ride of emotions. I can't live without Layna, Father. I don't even know how to pray for this. I pray for deliverance. I pray for her safe return to us. I know it's not going to be my will but Your will. Please, Father, I beg You, please don't let anything bad happen to her. Take me, Father. I will take her place. Just please don't let anything happen to her." I sit there and just cry. I really can't stop crying. I start thinking of my kids, and I really need to be strong for them. As I sit there thinking and tears still running down my cheeks, God reveals to me something. He reveals to me that this life here on Earth is as a vapor that is here for a short while and then vanishes away. We shouldn't place so much emphasis on this life.

I guess as a Christian, I can understand that. That doesn't necessarily make it easier to deal with a loved one being executed for their faith in Jesus Christ. However, there is a comfort in knowing that if that does happen, I know I will see her again one day soon.

Then my mind turns to all the things that we talked about in church, all the times we talked about the end and what the end might look like. I really feel like this is the end, and we are on the cusp of it all ending.

I get up to go meet Bob, and Dave decides to go with us too. We keep our numbers low so we don't draw too much attention to what we're doing. As we approach the courthouse, I can see an area where it looks like there is a lot of blood. I look at Bob and ask him, "What is going on here, and why is there so much blood everywhere?"

Bob replies hesitantly, "Since all of this has unfolded, they have performed public executions of people who are convicted of religious affiliation."

Clearly, these people mean business. We get into the courthouse, and we have to pass through a metal detector, and there are armed military as well as local law enforcement everywhere. I get into the courtroom, and it appears as though there are in the neighborhood of forty to fifty people who are standing before the judge for the same offense.

There she is. I can see Layna. Oh my goodness, she looks so tired and worried. She turns around and scans the room, and just like that, our eyes meet. She begins to weep, and I do too. I look at her with tears running down my face, and I tell her I love you. She smiles through the tears, and she tells me the same thing. I fold my hands as if I'm praying, and I signal to her to be praying. She nods in affirmation and does that right then and there.

"All rise! The honorable judge Tomkins presiding over court today!" I heard from countless people concerning their charge. Quickly and with prejudice, he finds each one guilty of federal law and sentences each one to death. I don't know what I'm going to do. She is in there with all of them, and the judge doesn't care about their side of the story. All he cares about doing is getting back to his golf outing or getting to go out on his lunch with his colleagues. There is no prejudice toward a specific faith. There are some from a little bit of all faiths present.

It's Layna's turn, and she stands before the judge. The judge asks her how she pleads, and she pleads not guilty. The judge asks, "So you are not guilty of a national crime involving religious contraband? There weren't copious religious items found in your residence? Are you telling me, ma'am, that you're not a Christian and that you had no religious contraband?"

Layna stands there quietly, knowing she's busted, and replies, "Yes, I did have all of those items. Yes, I am a Christian. Yes, I'm practicing my freedom of religion that I was afforded by my amendments. However, I'm not guilty of being a criminal. Having faith in my God is not a crime, no matter what the country calls it."

With no more discussion, the judge replies, "Okay, so you have admittedly and openly proclaimed you are a Christian and that you had those items, which you are no longer to possess under federal law. It is this court's decision that you're guilty, and you will be executed by statute of federal law."

I honestly feel like I am going to pass out. I feel my face gets hot and my heart palpitating. That's my wife! The love of my life! The person I was made for, and they are going to snuff her life out just like that? I look over at Bob and start talking, but nothing I am saying is coming out. I am crying so hard I can't say anything or do anything else. As I start quieting down, I realize there is a lot of crying in the room. Bob puts his arm around me and pulls me close to comfort me.

They start shuffling the convicted people outside into the courtyard. They line them up ten at a time. There are hundreds of people standing around, some are crying and others are laughing. Why would anybody laugh about this? We, as a people, have just lost some of the most important and protecting laws that we had. People are pointing and laughing, and some are making obscene gestures.

They line up, and I hear "Three . . . two . . . one . . . Fire!" Just like that, ten people are dead. Ten people are dead for living their life for their own deity. The next ten people line up, and I hear "Three . . . two . . . one . . . Fire!" As the blood fills the air and the gore from the executions mounts, I can hear the people watching getting more and more fired up about eradicating faith and religion from the face of the earth. The next ten line up. "Three . . . two . . . one . . . Fire!" As each ten is being executed, there are military soldiers who are ready to take the bodies and pile them up into the truck.

The next ten people are being shuffled into place. Layna is one of them this time. I'm still crying uncontrollably, and I can't contain it. Layna looks at me and blows me a kiss and lips the words "I love you." I keep saying "I love you," but it is messed up by my inability to speak right. She smiles at me as if to say she's ready to go. With what seems like an eternity and happens too quickly, "Three . . . two . . . one . . . FIRE!" I yell out, "NO!" Just like that, it is over. Her body falls lifeless to the ground, and I begin to black out. I can feel myself falling, and nothing I can do to stop it.

CHAPTER 7

I WAKE UP BACK at the headquarters, and I am lying in my bunk. I still can't process what happened. My beautiful wife is gone. Why did this have to happen, Father? Why didn't You protect her? I prayed for You to protect her, and she died! Father, I just need time to process this.

I sit up in the bunk and realize Jacob and Jessica are nowhere to be found. In a panic, I jump and begin yelling for them, "JACOB! JESSICA!"

A guy from another pod comes over and says, "Hey, are you looking for your kids? I was supposed to let you know that Mary is looking after them." So I begin to look around, and he points over there across the way. "See, there they are. They are doing okay."

I ask the guy who came up, "Do they know about my wife?"

He reluctantly replies, "I'm sorry to say, they don't. I'm so sorry for what you're going through. I lost my wife last year."

I exclaim, "You guys have been dealing with this stuff that long?"

The guy responds, "Oh no, my wife passed away last year from pancreatic cancer. It was a pretty tough time for me." Wow, how does one just lose a spouse and move on? The pain hurts so badly, and I don't think I can bear it any longer. He looks at me and says, "Hey, again, I'm sorry you're going through this. You don't have to go through this alone. I'm always available if you want to talk." I tell him thanks and then start walking toward my kids. "Hey!" he exclaims. I turn around, and he says, "My name is Stefan by the way." I wave and turn back around.

I'm usually a very nice and cordial person, but right now, I feel numb, and I certainly don't feel like being pleasant. I approach where Mary and my kids are, and Mary looks up at me. She has this sympathetic and sorry look on her face. I kneel, and I pull the kids in to me. "Hey, we need to go for a walk. Would you go for a walk with your dad?" They both nod yes. We get near the entrance of the headquarters where people are scarce. I say, "Listen, guys, I have something I need to tell you. It's not going to be easy to hear, but just know how much I love you and that we will be strong together if we stick together."

Jessica looks at me with tears in her eyes. "What's wrong, Dad? You're scaring me."

"Honey, Mom is gone. They arrested her, and she died yesterday."

Immediately, Jessica begins to cry. Jacob looks at me and says, "When will we get to see her again?"

As I begin to cry again, I tell him, "You'll get to see her again in heaven, buddy." I think Jacob understands at that point. He doesn't cry, but I think it's still sinking in to him.

We hear the dinner bell, and it is time to go get some food. I'm honestly still not hungry. I still feel like curling up into a ball and just dying. I can't do that though. I have to be strong for my two kids. They definitely need me to be strong.

I urge those two to go with Mary so that I can be alone for a bit. I walk outside the headquarters, and I just break down and begin to pray. "Father, how do I get through this? How can I be strong for them when I don't even know how to get through the night? I just feel like all the life, love, drive, and motivation in my life right now is gone. Layna was my better half and the person I spilled my heart to. I didn't even get to tell her 'Goodbye' or 'I love you.' I watched her executed right in front of me. How do I get that image out of my head? I desperately wanted to be there for her to know she wasn't dying alone, but I'm haunted by what I saw and the gruesomeness of it all. Father, I need Your strength . . . I need Your help! Amen."

I walk back inside after a good cry, and I grab my food. I happen to hear my name mentioned in a small circle that Bob happens to be a part of. I walk over to the circle, and Bob looks at me and then grabs me and gives me a solid hug. "Listen, buddy, I'm sorry you're going through this, and I'm sure you're sick of hearing that, but I'm here for you if you need to talk about anything. I also have a job for you that would involve your many talents, but go ahead and get through this, and we'll talk when the time is more appropriate." I look at him and nod yes. That's really all the positivity and affirmation that I can muster up.

I get into the line to grab something to eat. Mmmm, everybody loves cabbage stew. Yuck! I guess if you get hungry enough, you'll eat just about anything. I sit at the table that Mary and my kids are at. Mary looks at me and says, "Hey, John, this is Chad and Malissa, and they are sharing a pod with us." Chad looks over at me and says, "I know right. Cabbage is pretty nasty, but it was getting ready to go bad from sitting down here too long. Every once in a while, we have to eat stuff like this, but it's usually pretty good. You missed the good meal yesterday. We had chili yesterday, and that was good, but we were missing peanut butter bread." I smile to be nice, but I don't mutter a word. I'm tired and completely exhausted.

We get done eating, and I see Bob doing some cleaning up. "Hey, Bob," I mutter.

Bob replies, "Hey, brother, what's up?"

"I want to know what you have in mind for me," I ask.

Bob responds, "We can wait, John. It's definitely not a pressing matter, and it will be here for you when you're ready."

I slam my hand on the table and demand, "I heard what you said, but you didn't hear what I asked. I asked you what you have in mind for me!" Bob just looks at me, and of course, I feel like a jerk. Bob has been nothing but good to me. "I'm sorry, Bob. I have no excuse," I remorsefully assert.

Bob responds with a grin, "It's okay, John. I don't get offended easily. Why don't you sit down, and I'll explain it to you? As you know, we have our underground churches all over town, and the system that we're using is really inefficient. Basically, nobody knows where any of them are unless they get lucky and stumble upon one. So essentially, any new ones that we bring in, they tend to find one or two and then continue going to those until we're forced to move. However, for us to really make this work, we're going to need a new system. I like the markings to indicate 'X' marks the spot. However, for us to be effective at being ghosts, we're going to need to move around more and make it accessible for everybody to get to. Again, I don't know what you can do for us, but I want to see if you want to take the lead on this project. If you decide you don't want to, that's okay too, but I'm really hoping you'll take it. I think you need a distraction right now."

I look at Bob and tell him, "I'll take the job, and yes, I need a distraction. I'll let you know what I come up with." He nudges my arm, gets up, and continues to clean the mess hall.

I get back to my bed, and I notice the kids are already fast asleep. I feel so bad for them. How can I help them? I feel the Holy Spirit telling me that the best way I can help them is by staying strong, pressing into God, and making their lives better. How can I make this more efficient? Wait a second, this is the twenty-first century, and I'm a software designer. I know they are probably looking for something a bit simpler, but I can design software specifically for tracking underground churches. On the administrative side, I can make it so that any church location can be added or removed so that the user will be able to see active churches. I can use a map system similar to that of a car GPS to give me a layout of the city.

Now I can't get my brain to shut off. I think this can revolutionize the way we do things. Is it a perfect system? No. However, I think it's something we can fine-tune over time. I run back over to Bob, and I can see that he is just finishing cleaning the mess hall. "HEY! I have an idea, and I don't want to tell you anything until I can show you what I'm talking about. Do we have any computers down here that I can use?"

He looks at me with a smirk and a puzzled look and says, "Yes, we have two over there. The desktop computer isn't much to look at, but the laptop is a high-end laptop that was given to us by one of our people up top."

"I need permission to take the laptop so that I can create something that will blow your mind. Come on, you won't be sorry," I proclaim with confidence. He doesn't have the heart to say no. So I run over and grab the laptop, and in a flash, I'm back on my bed, developing something to make my life better, to make my kids' lives better, to make all Christians' lives better! Get ready. This is going to be great!

CHAPTER 8

MORNING QUICKLY ARRIVES, and I'm still up working on this software. Granted, I have been so occupied with getting this done I haven't really had much time to think about anything else. I know there is more pain and grief coming, but I need to stay focused on this right now.

My mind does wander at moments, and I think about the vacation our family took last year down to Orlando. We had such a great time. You know, most people are so much different when they're on vacations. Layna laughed so easy. She didn't struggle and fight through stress to smile. I wish I could kiss her again. I wish I could just touch her face one more time. My heart longs for her voice, her smell, her presence . . .

"Wait, stay focused, John. You can't do this right now," I assert to myself. So I take a quick drink and back to the software. I can see it coming together, and it's looking great, but there is still so much to do.

Bob walks by quietly as to not wake up the kids. "Hey, how's it going?" he asks.

"It's going pretty good, but it's coming pretty slow too," I reply.

Bob smiles and says, "I can imagine. I am looking at what you're doing there, and I have no idea what that is. In fact, it looks like somebody randomly smashing the keys on a keyboard."

As he laughs out loud, I ask, "Hey, do you know anybody down here or up top that either works on software or anything like that? Any kind of help I could get would sure help the process, but it has to be somebody you trust."

He nods and says, "Let me think about it. I think I might know somebody, but I want to be sure I'm thinking about the same thing." He puts his hand on my shoulder and walks away.

Jacob and Jessica wake up and come over and sit by me on my bed. Jacob asks, "Dad, did you go to sleep last night?"

"No, son, I've been working on this all night," I reply.

Jessica asks, "What is it that you're working on?"

I don't really want anybody to know yet because I'm not sure exactly if I can do it and if I can. I want it to be a surprise. "It's a surprise, honey. Say, why don't you take your brother over there and get some breakfast? I'll be over there soon, okay?" She nods, and they walk over to get breakfast.

About that time, Bob walks back up to me and says, "Hey, I think I know somebody that you can talk to about this. He does work up top, and I just called, and he's happy to help. He would like to see about meeting you for lunch to discuss what you have in mind. I don't know exactly what he does, but I know it has something to do with software. Also, his name is Adam May."

I ask, "Okay, where and what time?"

Bob replies, "Adam said to shoot for noon, and he said to shoot for Rosaline's café, just over there about six blocks from here. He also said he's happy paying because he knows you don't have much." I smile at Bob, and I thank him for helping me out.

I notice it's about 10:00 a.m. now, so I don't have a lot of time to get things together. I need to make sure he's onboard and see what I can assign him to do. So I sit and continue working and taking notes as to what I need him to work on.

About that time, I hear some yelling at the entrance of the headquarters. I quickly put down my laptop and rush over to see what's going on. When I get over there, a bunch of people are rushing in, and they are carrying this guy who has a gunshot wound to his back. Bob rushes over and asks what happened. They mention that he was shot for after they took off after being questioned about the Bibles they were carrying. Bob yells, "Elaine! We need you over here now!" I don't know who this Elaine is, but she seems to know what she's doing. I'm guessing she is some sort of nurse or doctor. It's so sad that it is coming to this. I wish there was more that I could do about this. I am making a contribution, but sometimes it just doesn't seem like enough.

I get my things together and ask that Mary look after Jacob and Jessica while I'm out. "Of course, it's no problem at all. It gives this old lady something to do." I sure do love Mary; she reminds me of my grandma. I give Jacob and Jessica a kiss, and I ask them to pray for me so that I can return safely.

I head out into the alley, and I think it's the first time I have seen the sun for days, but I'm not sure. My days seem to have blurred together after losing

Layna. Every time I get to thinking about Layna, I get inundated with more memories that were so perfect, like the time she made me this Father's Day present that was so awesome. She had like fifty balloons in the house as I walked in from work. Each balloon had a card tied to the end of it, and each card described things that she loved about me. As I got into the bedroom, most of the balloons were in there. Every time I moved, I would run into another balloon. I would read the cards, and I was just overrun with emotions. She loved me so much and so perfectly. I didn't deserve the kind of love she gave me. It just brings a smile to my face and a tear to my eye.

I start making the trek to the café, and I'm just keeping an eye out for anybody who may know me or completely avoiding military personnel. As I traverse the many blocks, I'm just overrun with sadness as I see so many things destroyed and so many people injured. What a sad state we have come to that would cause this great country to fall and that so many would find themselves staring down the end of a barrel because of their faith.

I finally make it to the café, and I walk in. I take a look around the room and look for somebody who might fit the description of a business type and software type. As I look around, I see nobody who matches that description. There is only one guy sitting by himself, but he looks more like somebody who was ripped out of a trailer park from the 1980s. I take a chance, and I walk up to him. "Hi. Are you Adam by chance?" I ask.

He looks up at me and smiles. "Yep, that's me!" Seriously, he looks just like somebody I know.

I take a seat and ask him, "So Bob told me that you might be able to help me with a software project that I'm working on. Is that true?"

He replies, "Absolutely! I love working on software! So how much does this job pay?"

"This job doesn't pay anything. I'm creating a program that I'm giving away for free, and I'm not taking any pay for it," I reply.

He exclaims, "Wait a second, I'm not making any money on this project?"

I respond, "No, I'm sorry. I thought you knew that this project was no pay."

He begrudgingly replies, "No, I don't have time for a free project. I'm already very busy and not making enough money as it is."

"Wait!" I exclaim. "Please hear me out. Are you a Christian?" I ask.

"Yes," Adam says.

I reply, "Then help me make a difference for the lives of thousands of people. Yes, I can do it on my own, but it would take me so much longer, and right now, time is not on our side. Please help me make a difference in the world."

He looks at me and purses his lips and agrees to help me. I sit there for quite some time explaining what I'm doing, and I'm giving him little projects that he can work on to implement into my program. He understands exactly what I'm doing and is happy to help.

I get up from a very lengthy discussion, and he smiles and shakes my hand. Just like that, he is out the door. I feel really good about the direction this meeting went, and I'm very excited about what we're going to do to revolutionize this country and the rest of the world.

I start my journey back to the headquarters, and the sun is going down. This side of town, there aren't many streetlights that actually work. Since all this went down, I have seen many local governments roll up the carpet and close the town down.

I'm only a block or so from the entrance to the headquarters now, so I'm feeling better about getting in from outside. As I start making my way around the corner, I can feel somebody walking behind me. I glance over my shoulder and see somebody in the corner of my eye, but I can't tell who it is. What if it's an undercover officer or something? I can't take the risk of heading for the entrance when somebody is watching me. So I continue walking as if I have somewhere else I need to go. As I continue walking, I can hear their steps hasten, and they are getting closer. I do a full turn around this time, and I can see three men approaching me. I take off running, and I'm outpacing them a little bit. I'm darting in and out of alleys as well as abandoned buildings.

In a flash, I accidentally drop my laptop, and it lands in a puddle of water. "Oh NO!" I shout. If anybody knows anything about electronics, they know water and electronics do not mix. I think I may have just lost everything that I have been working on, but it looks like I may have outmaneuvered my followers. So I start making my way back to the entrance, but this time I take the long route. As I approach the entrance, I stand there for a few minutes to determine whether I'm alone. I don't see anybody, but I can hear a couple of guys not too far away. So without delay, I get into the entrance to the headquarters and make my way in.

I can't believe I dropped my laptop. I hope I didn't lose anything. I'm shaking the laptop, trying to ensure all the water is out of it. I'm not going to take any chances. I'm going to put it on my bed and allow the water to drain out of it and ensure any remaining water is evaporated.

I put the laptop on my bed and leave it sitting there without powering it on. I want to ensure I don't make things worse by trying to fire it up and then shorting out the motherboard.

As I'm sitting on the bed, I realize I have nothing to do. This is a problem because with nothing to occupy me, I get to thinking about Layna again. I grab what little stuff I had of hers, and I start going through it. I see her purse in there, and I start going through it. There is the picture we took at the restaurant on her birthday. I could feel myself being to cry. I just miss her so much. There is a folded piece of paper in the purse, but it's yellow and looks like something she would have been given and not necessarily something that she made. I look at the paper, and it is from her doctor's office. As I read down the paper, it says that she tested positive for pregnancy. I can feel my heart actually hurt. Why didn't she tell me? I look at the date on the paper, and it was the two days before that Sunday when everything fell apart that my wife found out she was pregnant. I begin to cry again, and I'm just overwhelmed with sadness again. It's as if the scab was picked off, and I'm bleeding all over again. My wife was pregnant . . .

CHAPTER 9

WHY WOULDN'T SHE tell me? I assume with everything that went down, it just didn't seem like the right time. As I sit and think about it, I begin to feel as though that was such a heavy burden that she was carrying. She didn't complain or feel sorry for herself. Her only concern was to ensure that her family was safe. All of a sudden, my mind is taken back to a brief moment before I left the hotel room when she told me she had something that she wanted to talk to me about. We never got that moment to talk. I will never allow anything to prevent me from talking to the people I love again.

I decide to lie down and try and get some sleep. I feel so stressed out My wife was killed, I just found out she was pregnant, the work I was doing on the laptop could be gone and the laptop might be ruined, and I'm down in a hole in the ground with my kids. My life is just a mess right now. I understand that everybody's life is a mess right now, but everybody's circumstances are different. I decide to just go ahead and close my eyes and maybe I'll dream about times when my life was better.

I go outside and walk downtown by the courthouse. I see the posts and the blood on the ground where my wife was killed. As I look around, it is dark and depressing. I can feel a strange presence around me, but I can see absolutely nothing. There isn't a soul in sight. I notice out of the corner of my eye something moving. I turn my head to look, and it's my wife. I can feel my mouth opening uncontrollably and tears forming in my eyes. I yell, "LAYNA! What are you doing?" She appears to be standing in a gateway and across a chasm to which I can't reach her. I approach, and she looks at me with a smile. "I love you, babe . . . Take care of our precious kids."

I can feel the tears running down my cheeks as I desperately want to just hold her. I can feel myself reaching for her, but no matter how hard I push, she is always just outside my reach. As she turns to walk away, I see a small child run up to her and leap into Layna's arms. I see Layna kiss her and give her a big hug and points toward me and say, "Look, precious . . . that's Daddy." The glimpse fades.

Then I see something horrible. I see millions of people worshipping an idol, and this idol is high above them. I see what seems like a mark upon this person, but I can feel the presence of evil all around him. Just right after noticing these things, I see a nuclear bomb falling from the sky. As I look around, I see what seems like hundreds of nuclear bombs falling from the sky. I was standing on a grassy knoll just outside a large city. I gather my kids to me and pull them close. I tell them, "This is the end. Pray hard, and we'll be in heaven soon." As the bombs detonate, I can feel the intensity of the light and the heat of that light on my body. After the light of the blast finally subsides, I can see this massive explosion. This explosion seems to touch the atmosphere; it is so high. I can see the fire approaching me, and right before, the blast gets to me.

I quickly sit up in bed and realize it was all a dream. I sit and cry about seeing Layna and how I could touch her. I think that child was ours. I believe that was the one she was pregnant with. All I can do is smile; it was a girl. What a dream that was! That was so scary and seemed so real. What did it mean? I have never seen a nuclear explosion like that in real life, but I have seen them on television. I'm telling you, that never felt so real.

I look at the clock, and it's about 4:00 a.m. I look around the room, and most people are sleeping. I notice Mary is sitting up watching some movie on her little nine-inch television. I get up and start walking over. As I approach, I see her looking at me, and she begins to smile. "Pull up a chair and talk to me," she says while turning the television down.

As I am still drying the tears off my face and my eyes, I say, "Mary, I can't tell you how much I have appreciated you looking out for my kids while I have been going through this. It really means a lot."

Mary replies, "It's absolutely my pleasure, but just remember, they are suffering too. They also need some dad time."

I nod in agreement. "Hey, can I ask you a question? Are you any good with dreams?" I ask.

She replies, "Well, I'll tell ya what. Sometimes I am, and sometimes I'm not."

With a puzzled look, I ask her, "Okay, so how do I know when it is that you'll be any good with dreams?"

She responds smugly, "Well, when the Holy Spirit tells me, then I'll know." I smile, and she smiles right back at me.

So I proceed to tell her about my dream and all the little details that made this dream seem so real. I know she can sense the emotion in my face and in my voice. She just soaks up all that I'm telling her, and even a couple of times, she closes her eyes as if to soak up everything that I'm saying. Truthfully, a couple of times, I really thought she was sleeping.

She opens her eyes and says, "Listen, honey, that is a crazy dream. However, I promise you one thing, if anybody knows anything about this dream, God will. I'll tell you what I'll do. I'll pray about it, and I'll tell you what God tells me about it. How does that sound?"

I really don't have many other options. My dream was definitely crazy, but I'm sure she's right, God will probably be the only one who will know anything about this dream. "That sounds great, Mary! I really appreciate your listening to my crazy dream and helping me out with the kids through all of this," I remark.

She replies, "As I said, this old lady has nothing to do anyways, so I'm happy to help. I'm sorry you're going through this, but remember, there is a light at the end of the tunnel. Stay focused, and one day God will narrow that chasm and will make it easy for you to just step right across."

I get back up and head back over to my bunk. I sit, and I begin looking right at the laptop. I wonder if all the moisture in the laptop is all out yet. I wonder if the laptop is still usable. I don't have the heart to tell Bob yet that I might have ruined this expensive laptop. If it's ruined, I'm going to have to put a halt to what I'm working on until we can get a new one. Lesson learned, though, no more taking the laptop anywhere. So I grab up the laptop and give it just a wee little shake. I can't hear anything in there, and I don't see any water falling out. So I decide to take the leap and try to fire it up.

I slowly put my finger toward the button, and I can feel my heart racing. At the same time, I am asking for God to help start the laptop. I know how that sounds, but I really need God's help right now. I really don't want to tell Bob I ruined the only laptop we have down here, and I really don't relish the idea of starting over on the program that I had started. I had many good ideas, and I think I might have a hard time remembering all the ideas that I put into the software. So as my finger is touching the button now, I close my eyes and quickly press the button.

Ahhh, the sound of a humming laptop never sounded so good. Other than the typical "You didn't shut windows down properly" screen, it comes up like business as usual. Praise God! I get back in there, and all my stuff is still there, waiting for me. So like an excited little schoolboy with enough money in his pocket for chocolate, I begin working feverishly on the ideas that I was thinking about before and some of the ideas that Adam and I brainstormed about over lunch. This is going to be amazing, and I can't wait for everybody, including my kiddos, to see the finished product. I think they will appreciate what I have done, and they'll be proud of what I have accomplished. It will make everything seem worth it.

CHAPTER 10

WELL, TEN O'CLOCK rolls around, and I can hardly believe I have been working on this for several hours since I turned it back on. I'm so thankful that this laptop turned on. Jacob and Jessica are up and ready to go. I look at them. "Why are you two dressed up and ready to go, and where did you get those clothes?"

Jessica responds, "These are some of the clothes that Mary gave us. They are pretty nice, huh?"

"Yes, but you didn't tell me where you're going," I repeat.

Jacob responds, "Dad, today is Sunday. We're going to church!"

Wow, it really is Sunday, and it feels like an eternity since I have been in church. So much has happened since we were in church last. When we were in church last, my whole family was there with smiles on their faces and joy in our hearts. I just feel tired and sad in my soul. I know that's where I need to be though.

I jump out of bed and put the laptop down. I look through my clothes; however, nothing is too fancy in my lot of clothes. So I put on what I have that's best. I get all ready to go, and I approach Mary. "Hey, where are most of us going today for church?"

Mary look at me with a smile, and her head slightly tilts. "Well, we all go to our own places or wherever we have been going. If you haven't been going anywhere yet, you're welcome to come with me to mine." Sounds good enough. I don't really have a set place to go anyway, and of course, Mary has been so good to me. It just seems like the right thing to do.

"We'll walk out, and we're only over about five blocks, so it will be a quick walk," Mary announces. So we walk out, and it is such a nice day. The sun is shining, the birds are singing, and the temperature outside is just wonderful. Truthfully, though, I'm a little gun shy about being outside. So much bad has happened, and I don't want to lose the little bit of family I have left.

There is still so much smoke in the air in some places though. I wonder if this town will ever get back to a state of normal. The streets are littered with homeless and wandering people. My heart really hurts for them. Are they Christian? Do they even believe? I guess it doesn't really matter; a person just hates seeing other humans live this way. I wonder what is being done to minister to these people on the street and what can we do for them. I remember the conversation Bob and I had about the headquarters being filled to the maximum, and there are a couple of other safe zones in Philly, but they are pretty full too. Clearly, moving them into the headquarters really isn't an option, but maybe there is something else that can be done.

I notice in the distance some military, maybe National Guard, cleaning up some of the debris and rubble from riots and damage from grenades. I'm sure the government wants this all swept under the rug as if nothing has changed. That's messed up because everything has changed. Some people look at what has happened and say this can be a good thing; we will be able to eliminate the bad elements in religion. That's true, but what about the good elements? What about our amendments and our rights to freedom of religion? If one of our rights and freedoms is so easily thwarted, who's to say that the others can't just be removed just like these?

We begin to walk down an alley, and I notice a manhole cover that is slightly off. Mary looks at me and says, "We're here. It's just down there." I look around to see where the marker is, but I'm not seeing it.

"Hey, Mary, how would a normal person know that there is a meeting here?" I ask.

She replies, "Actually, you really have to look. If you'll take about five steps back, you'll see the answer." So I take about five steps back and notice the mark on the side of a dumpster. Mary responds, "See, this is the best system we have, but it will at least let you know that you're close." I just nod and start making my way to the manhole cover. I hope to change the system that we have in place one day very soon.

We get underground, and it really doesn't smell all that bad, or maybe I'm just used to the nasty smell that usually emanates from the sewers I have been frequenting. I'm sure it's just to throw people off our "scent."

As we get in the room where the church is, I notice there are about ten people down there. I turn to Mary and ask, "Where is everybody? This doesn't seem like very many people."

She replies, "John, you're going to have to retrain and rethink what you see in your head about church. The days of churches running fifty to one thousand people are over. We have to keep our numbers low so we don't get noticed. Actually, we normally don't have this many. We have two other visitors today."

This little place is very small. I would say if you could fit twenty people down here, I would be shocked. There is one light bulb in the middle of the room, and it's really dim for the amount of area that has to be lit. It actually is set up a lot like a church but just a much smaller scale. I look around the room and see no musical instruments and no piano. This place is definitely not much to look at; in fact, it's pretty gross.

"John, don't focus on the appearance of where we are. Focus on meeting with our family and focus on God right now. You'll get used to being in places like this. Just give it time," Mary whispers.

So this guy up front starts speaking from the Bible and then pauses for prayer. As we finish prayer, everybody grabs a folder with papers from the back of the chair in front of them, and they begin to sing quietly. So we're nearly whispering our songs, and we have no music. There is a compilation of hymn songs and contemporary songs in these little folders. Maybe I am placing too much emphasis on where I worship. Maybe I have become spoiled about where I worship and how I do so. I'm so used to those cushiony chairs, climate-controlled, and good-smelling churches that I became accustomed to.

As I sit there thinking about all this, my mind turns back to some of the petty little arguments that some found so important. I don't like this air freshener, I don't like these curtains, and I don't like this wall color. Once you get into a situation like this, you would gladly take any walls, in any color, with any curtains, and I guarantee it would smell a far sight better than this smelly sewer. I'm so ashamed of how we reacted to petty things like this and sad about how God felt looking down on us arguing about such foolish things. We had it made up top and didn't even realize it.

This guy speaking is not good, but I commend him for at least trying. I lean over to Mary and ask her with a smirk on my face, "What's up with this guy? Does he even know what he's doing?"

Mary whispers back, "He just started about a week or so ago. His father was the one doing it before him."

Trying to be funny, I mention, "Well, we need to see about getting his dad back up there."

Without a smile, she leans over and says, "I'm sure he would love that . . . His dad was killed last week by militant forces."

Oh my goodness, I feel foolish. What was once normal and sometimes even funny has dramatically changed. I shouldn't have said that. Truthfully, I don't even know if I would have had the strength he has to be doing what he is doing after his dad got killed not more than a week ago.

Ironically, the message we have today is about making the best of what you have and allowing God to use you in any situation. Even though we are in this situation, that doesn't mean God is dead and cannot use anybody. If anything, this is the time for us to press in and allow God to draw as many people to Him as possible. I really need to change quite a few things about the way I think. I only hope one day I'm as dedicated as this guy is standing in front of us.

We dismiss, and I walk up to the speaker, and I shake his hand. He looks at me and says, "You must be new. I haven't seen you before. I'm sorry, I wasn't quite on my 'A' game, but I'm still adjusting. My name is Dan, by the way."

I introduce myself, "You did good, Dan. I'll be back for more next time. My name is John, and this is my daughter, Jessica, and my son, Jacob." He nods and shakes their hands. I also mention, "By the way, you really can hit those notes. I could hear you sing, although not that loud, but you're really good."

Dan responds, "Thanks. I appreciate that. Before all this went down, I was thinking about pursuing a singing career, but I never did. I wish I would have done so when I had the chance."

I look at Dan and smile. "You never know. God may still use that gift He gave you yet."

We shook hands and parted company. We begin making our way back to the headquarters, and I am just blown away by how much I don't know. Everything has changed, and these people seem to have evolved overnight. I feel like I just crawled out from beneath a rock, and I'm learning everything that they already know. It's time to rethink a great many things.

CHAPTER 11

I GET BACK TO the headquarters, and after what I experienced at church, I have more resolve now to finish the software than ever before. However, I remember what Mary told me, my kids do need me too. So as we are walking in from outside, I ask the kids, "Hey, what would you two say about playing a board game with your dad?" Of course, their eyes light up and are all too happy to do anything with me. They both respond in unison, "Yes!" So we walk over to the games, and we see our all-time favorite game. We begin to play, and I see them smile and laugh, and I haven't seen that from them since before Layna was gone. It truly is good medicine for our souls. At this moment, I have such great pride in being a dad and doing everything I can to keep my kids safe.

We play for what seems like hours. After it is all done, I look at Jessica and say, "Hey, why don't you and I go for a walk?"

She responds, "Sure, that sounds good." I sent Jacob over to watch some TV, and Jessica and I begin to walk. We stay inside, but we are walking around the perimeter where we have some privacy.

I look at Jessica and ask her, "How are you doing, sweetheart? I know so much has happened, and it's a lot to deal with. Talk to me and tell me what's going on with you."

She looks at me and begins to cry. I wait to see what she will say. "Dad, I have been trying to hold it together for too long. I feel like our family is falling apart. I never got to even say goodbye to Mom! I never got to tell her that I love her. I never got to ask her if she's proud of me," Jessica mumbles through the tears.

I pull her in close to me and say, "Listen, honey, your mom loved you very much, and she would have done anything for you. Your mom has always been proud of you. Even before all this stuff went down, you were always somebody whom your mom respected and was proud of. Listen, sweetie, your mom knew that you loved her very much. It was evidenced by the way you spoke to her, showed her, and you told her all the time. We will get to see your mom again. We just have to hang on and stay on course." As she is wiping away the tears, she smiles, and I knew at that moment she believes everything I told her. "Listen, you can come and talk to me anytime you want, okay?" I add. She nods in affirmation, and then I say, "Also, I'm working on something I think will make you proud of your dad, so give me time. I know it's taking time away from you and your brother, but this is so important, and you will see what it is when I'm done."

She smiles and says, "Dad, I'm always proud of you! I can't wait to see what it is."

I pull her to my side, and we continue to walk together for a bit longer. I then tell her, "Okay, honey, I'm going to have to get on what I'm working on. I just wanted to spend a little time with my favorite daughter."

She replies with sarcasm, "Okay, Dad, I know I'm your favorite daughter. I would be even if you had two." I smile, and then we part company.

Okay, so back to the software. This is going to take some time to finish. It just dawned on me we have no way to run this software, and if we're going to run it for mobile devices or computers, we're going to have to have it hosted on a server out of the country. We certainly don't have the money to buy a server and can't host it in the United States given the new laws that have taken effect. Either way, I control my ADD long enough to get back on the software. I need to present this to Bob to see what he thinks. So I approach Bob and say, "Hey, Bob, this is really important. We need to talk. Do you have a few minutes?"

Bob looks at me with excitement and concern and replies, "Sure, what do you need?" I begin to show him and explain to him what this software really is and what it can do.

So I have the software compiled and really getting it together. Let me tell you what it is. This software is going to revolutionize the way Christians meet, and it will afford opportunities for other Christians to find one another without having to worry too much about getting caught or keeping symbols outside that others can learn about and then find. If the military figure out what these symbols mean, it will be the quickest way of finding all Christians and killing them as quickly as possible.

The software will be set up by region, so for example, I will have a "site master" for Philadelphia who will allow a person to give access to any Christian in that area. I will be able to set up editors and users. The editors will be able to put their meeting location on their log-on so that others in the area will be able to see what is available for meetings. It will be available 24/7 and 365 days a year, so we won't have to worry about meeting just on Sunday; we can meet all week if we want to. The editor will also have the ability to mark the location as full if enough people show up, so others will be able to make different arrangements. This is going to make switching locations a breeze, and we won't have to worry anymore about the wrong locations falling into the wrong hands.

So this can be accessed from a computer or a smartphone. The app will also be disguised as a photo editor, and once you get in there, there will actually be photo editing abilities. However, to get in there, you will need either to provide a password or use some element of biometrics that most smartphones have nowadays. Once inside, to access the actual location part, one would simply need to click on the help button three times, and that would bring up another password or biometric function. Once inside, the user will have access to all meeting locations within that region. The software is called Ma tovu ohalecha, which, translated from Hebrew, means "How fair are your tents," which comes from the words of Balaam in Numbers 24:5 in the Bible. It was his time to speak curses to the Israelites but rather chose to speak blessings.

I know what you're thinking, and you're absolutely right—it's not 100 percent. It can still be hacked or fall into the wrong hands. However, it's a better system than the one we currently have set up. There is a much higher propensity that this will keep Christians safer for longer. If the region ever becomes compromised, I can change the master password, and everybody's password would change, and they would have to see whoever I have set up to govern that area.

I explain all this to Bob, and his mind is literally blown. He cannot even believe what I'm working on. He looks at me in shock and says, "Wow, I didn't even have a clue that you were working on something like this. You have to roll this out everywhere." That's a really good idea. I never thought about rolling this out everywhere, but that could be the very thing that God protected me for.

I look at Bob and ask him, "Would you be interested in governing this area? If I'm going to make this available to other areas, I'm going to need to make my way around and ensure everybody has access to this."

He replies, "Absolutely. You just tell me what you need from me, and I will do whatever you need."

I look at him with a smile and remark, "Okay, I'm going to be rolling this out, but Philly will be my test area, and we are going to see how effective it is here first. You know, kind of use Philly as my guinea pig."

He nods with a smile and says, "I think this will change our lives!"

So I start making preparations to roll this out, and I decide to have the software hosted in Switzerland. The website is safe there as they have no laws concerning religion, and they are fairly technology savvy, so it should be secure.

Hmm, having this software hosted there is going to require some money. Money I don't have. I have to think about that one. In the meantime, I can keep on building the software and putting the final touches on what I have. I can always update it as I go.

Within the software, I set myself up as the designer, and I have a full and unlimited access to the software. I can add or remove governors, editors, and users at will. I set Bob up as a governor, and I will just need to show him how this works.

In the process of a full-on ADD meltdown, Mary walks up to me and says, "Hey, if you have a minute, I think I know what God wants you to know about your dream."

I look at her, undoubtedly with bloodshot eyes and a forlorn look on my face, and reply, "Yeah, that sounds great. What do you have?"

Mary tells me, "I'm going to start with the second part of your dream first. When you were standing there on the knoll and you saw an explosion. This symbolizes the end of all things. The end will come, and you will need to be ready. However, the dream also reveals that sin was running rampant and that men and women were turning to their evil ways and evil desires. I believe this is where we are starting, and it will get so much worse before it's all over. However, the first part was interesting. God revealed to me that your purpose is going to make you feel alone, and it will be a lonely ministry. Evil will be around you all the time. However, keep your eyes fixed on what matters the most to you. Getting to see God, heaven, and your lost loved ones will be the motivating factor in fulfilling the purpose that God has for you. Believe me, it's a great purpose and a great mission that God has for you. Don't be afraid to pursue it, and don't give up. It's worth it all in the end. That's it, honey. That's all I was given. I hope that helps you in your situation."

Before I even had a chance to say anything, she walks away. This is clearly what God is talking about. The same thing that Mary told me, the same thing that Bob had mentioned, and the same thing I have felt compelled to do since I started designing this software. I have a long mission ahead of me.

CHAPTER 12

I FINALLY HAVE THE software ready to go, and I think with some training, I can roll out Philadelphia pretty quick. I have made some finishing touches on the software that I think will make this Christian network really versatile and, at the same time, allow many Christians places to go.

I approach Bob again. "Hey, Bob, I need to talk again. Do you have a few minutes?" He is eager to help because he really feels like this software is going to revolutionize the underground church.

Bob replies, "Of course. What's up?"

"Well, I need your help. I am going to be doing some training with you as I'm setting you up as the governor for Philadelphia. I think you're somebody that everybody trusts, and I think you are well networked. However, that isn't why I've come to talk to you today. I need about six computers as well as about $1,000 to start, and I need to set up a training schedule and volunteers that will want to help with this endeavor. Do you think you can help get us going?" I ask.

Bob looks at me with a surprised expression and says, "Whoa, six computers and $1,000? That's going to be tough."

I reply, "Look, I get it. You're the most well-connected person in town that I know of. I know it's not going to be easy, but we really need this stuff, and we need it yesterday. Please help me, Bob."

Bob smiles and looks at me and says, "Of course, I'll help. I'll do whatever I can. Give me forty-eight hours, and I will let you know my game plan."

I pat Bob on the shoulder, smile, and then walk away. I know Bob will do whatever he can do, and I know he is well connected. I know at this point it's just a waiting game to see what we can come up with. My goal is to ensure this software is absolutely ready to be uploaded to the server to ensure we have no wasted time once it's paid for.

It's getting late, and I don't feel like I have slept much the last few days. With everything happening and what has happened, I just haven't slept very well. It's not every day this kind of thing happens. I mean, just a matter of weeks ago, I was living a normal life without a care in the world. Everything was just fine. Now my whole world is upside down, and my beautiful wife is dead. It's just a lot to deal with.

I tuck Jacob and Jessica in, and I put myself in bed. I lie there thinking about the software and how I am going to roll this thing out. My brain is literally going a hundred miles per hour, and I can't seem to shut it off. Not only that, but I also feel like I'm three steps ahead in my brain of where God wants me. My only option is to pray and see where God leads me.

I pray, "Father, this has been a tough day. I thank You so much for Your grace and Your strength. Father, I need this every single day. I cannot make it without You. Father, my brain is going so fast, and I don't want to get ahead of You. I know when that happens, nothing will turn out correctly. Please pace me, Father. Give me a sense of urgency, but help me to keep it in Your time! I need direction here, Father. I want the whole world to experience what I have made with Your help, but it needs to be done correctly. Help to shut my brain down tonight so that I can get some rest. I lift these things up to You, Father, and I pray for Your divine intervention. In Jesus's name, I pray and Amen!"

I am going from place to place, and I remember teaching people about this software. There is much rejoicing and a whole lot of satisfaction knowing this software is making their lives easier. I remember standing in front of a large number of people, and I can hear them cheering for me and clapping. As I look to my right, I can see my wife again standing across this great chasm. I try yelling to her, but the cheering and clapping are so loud she would have never heard me. I can see her and the same child she had with her before. However, the skies grow dark, and I remember the phone that I have in my hand with the software on it has melted away. I remember seeing this man, and he looks evil. He starts running toward me, and no matter how fast I ran, he is gaining on me. Every time I look back at him, he is so much closer. Up ahead of me, I can see this beautiful and brilliant light. I am racing and running as fast as I can toward this light. However, this evil man keeps gaining on me. Right before he grabs me, I wake up.

I sit straight up in bed, and I am drenched in sweat. I have no idea what that was all about, but it was very scary. I look over at Mary, and I can see she is up watching television. So I start making my way over there to talk to her. I say, "Mary, do you ever sleep?"

She replies, "Well, I do from time to time. You know something, sleep isn't what it's cracked up to be, and truthfully, it's not what it used to be." I just can't help but laugh.

I ask her, "Would you have time to hear about the dream I just had?"

She snickers and looks at me. "I don't need to! God was telling me about your dream while you were sleeping, and I'm ready to tell you what it means."

"Are you serious?" I ask.

She responds, "I'm very serious! God's work is something I never joke around about. So He has an ear, let Him hear! I don't know what you're doing or what you're working on, but God wants you to know that it's going to be a great success and is so desperately needed in the world today. He wanted me to tell you that you are going to be responsible for sharing this with the world. He wants you to know that you should keep your eyes fixed on Him. He doesn't want what happened to Peter stepping off the boat to happen to you. Keeping your eyes fixed on Him will get you the ending you want and the eternity you need. However, Satan is going to be on your back side every step of the way. The days are going to get dark for you, and tragedy will continue to find you, but take comfort in knowing that you are not alone. You see, death finds us all, but this brief life isn't worth all this struggling to hang on to. Everything that is going to happen is a means to an end, and the end is graduation day. Don't let Satan get the best of you. Keep your eyes on that bright light, and all will be fine. Does this answer your question?"

I am in total shock. I have heard of miracles, and I have seen some miracles, but I have never seen God use somebody like He uses Mary. I respond in sheer amazement, "You're an amazing woman, Mary! I'm so happy that God placed you in my life. That is exactly what I needed to hear, and I'm on the cusp of rolling this software out to make the lives of Christians better everywhere."

She smiles and says, "God is using you in miraculous ways. Just remember what I said. Things are going to get bad for you, and you might even think you're suffering alone. However, there are many suffering right alongside you, and there are many great people that have suffered the same that have gone on before you. Take comfort in that and know I will be praying for you and will be here anytime you need me."

I give Mary a hug and make my way back to my area. As I sit on my bunk processing everything that Mary had just told me, I realize that everything will be fine. Hmmm, is that pancakes I smell? This ADD is sometimes inconvenient, but I suppose I am the way I am for a reason.

I walk over there, and a few people have started eating. I grab some food and sit and say a little prayer. "Father, thank You so much for the great dream and, furthermore, the great interpretation. I thank You for sending so many great people in my path. I just pray that You continue to lead this, and I lay it at Your feet. This is the only way that I can guarantee the success of this program. I also thank You for a roof over my head, clothes on my back, and food in my belly. Bless this food for which I'm about to eat. Amen."

I sit there eating these pancakes with a smile on my face. I know this software is going to be a huge success, and I know if I keep my eyes fixed on God, I will see my beautiful wife again soon.

CHAPTER 13

I FINISH EATING BREAKFAST, and I see Bob out of the corner of my eye. He sort of skips over to me and says, "Hey, I have some great news!"

I respond, "Wow, it hasn't even been forty-eight hours! That's great!"

He smiles and says, "Okay, so I have the money! A couple businessmen from up top are still working and making good money. They have offered the $1,000 that you requested. They also told me they could get us three computers tomorrow and another three computers in a week!"

I cannot believe it! Not only did God provide the money we needed but the computers that we needed as well! I look at Bob in shock and reply, "Wow! You're awesome, and praise God that He saw the need and made it happen."

Bob says, "Okay, so I have the $1,000 on a prepaid Visa card, so here you go. Do what you can do! If I didn't believe in this project, I wouldn't have fought so hard to get what we need."

This is absolutely great news. I take the visa card over to my little work area and slap my laptop up on the table. Within an hour, I have the server set up in Switzerland, and everything is running as it should be. I have everything encrypted correctly, and I feel like this is going to be a safe website for Christians everywhere to use.

"Hey, Bob, can you come here for a minute?" I ask. Bob comes over to where I'm working, and I explain to him what a governor of the software does. I explain that he is the sole authority for Philadelphia; however, he's also the leader of the little call-in station for the program. I show him on the tablet and the smart phone where people have access. I explain to him why people will be messaging in, and they will have to have security questions in place to prevent unauthorized access. Bob and his team will have access to ALL areas and their own access password. This way, anybody passing through can verify who they are and then find out where church services will be without actually gaining access to the entire area network. This limits the access of people who shouldn't have access to the entire area.

Bob acknowledges everything that I explain. I figure he will do just fine. You see, he used to be a white-collar executive of a large company here in Philly. Then everything went south, and that was all there was left to it. So needless to say, he understands computers and software. Everything is set up and ready to go, and I tell Bob, "Okay, make up a password for this area. It's your responsibility to ensure every user and editor has access and that they understand how this works. It's your best bet to teach the editors and then let them teach the users. This might expedite the training and cut down on the learning time." He quickly acknowledges. I mention, "Bob, I'm going to have to leave. I have to share this with the world. There are so many Christians out there that need something like this. They need to continue having service, and they don't necessarily know how they're going to do it."

Bob replies, "I kind of figured that's what you were going to do. Are you sure you need to go?"

I acknowledge, "Unfortunately, there is no other way. I will probably not be back here again. I will be leaving in the morning to start my journey."

He smiles and says, "I understand. Let's let everybody know so we can have a little celebration tonight and say farewell." I agree to do that.

I just realize, since all this went down, it has been two and a half months. It is nearly July now, and I'm really not sure where all the time went. It has been two weeks since Layna was executed, but it also feels like it was just yesterday. It definitely still feels fresh.

The word at the headquarters spread quickly that me and my family are leaving. We have made some great friends and met some really great people since we have been here in Philly. It hurts my heart to lose them and walk away from them. They got me through a lot of hurt, and I can honestly say they are what Christians should be like.

As everybody gather together, they bring out cake and ice cream to celebrate. There is music and laughing, much like what I would expect it would have been like before all these horrible things happened. Bob stands in front of everybody and says, "Listen, everybody. For those of you who many not know, John and his kids are going to be leaving us. They are going to be doing God's work and ensuring that God's people have the ability to meet up with each other and worship like God intended. I, for one, am sad to see them go.

However, I believe and take comfort in knowing they are doing His will, and I will see them again, one way or another. I will be praying that we get to see them again on this side of heaven, but if not, I pray God's peace and strength follow this family wherever God leads them."

I can see some tears and some smiles, and it makes my heart feel good to know that we have a kinship with these people that can never be taken away. I stand with Bob and say, "Thank you, Bob, for all your help and support. As many of you know, this last couple of weeks for my family have been very tough with my wife being gone. God has definitely laid this on my heart to ensure others can benefit from it. Will I pay the ultimate price? I truthfully don't know. What I do know is this, Jesus paid the ultimate price for us and laid down His life for us. I have to be willing to do the same thing for all of you. As Bob has mentioned, I don't know if I will be back, but I appreciate and love you very much. Please pray for us. I believe we will need all the prayers we can get."

After our little speeches, we just turn on the music and spend some time dancing, eating, even did a little praying with some. I have to say, for what little we have, it is a great going-away party. The cake is simply divine. I honestly think I forget what cake tastes like, but it is marvelous!

As things wind down for the day and everybody thins out and goes back to their area, I am face-to-face with the quietness of this big room. All I have to keep me companion are my thoughts–thoughts of Layna, thoughts of trials and tribulations, and thoughts of death. You know, the kinds of things a person thinks about before the end. When will all this go down? I don't know.

As I am pondering, I look up, and I see Mary sitting on her bunk holding her Bible. As she turns her head and looks at me, she smiles and points at me. She then motions for me to come over to her. Of course, she's just like my grandma. How could I say no?

I sit, and she starts off by saying, "Tomorrow is the big day, huh? This is the direction that God has for you?"

I reply, "I believe so. I believe this is going to change the life of so many people, don't you?"

She responds with a tear rolling down her cheek. "Well, if God is telling you to do this, then yes, I believe it really will change the life of many people. However, there's something I want you to know. I look at you like my family. I have grown so attached to your kids. You see, I never had kids. Doctor said I couldn't have kids. I never got to experience what it was like to have kids or grandkids. If I could have chosen kids or grandkids, I would have chosen you and your kids. Would you mind if I pray with you?"

As I feel tears rolling down my face, I reply, "I don't mind."

Mary proclaims, "Dear Lord Jesus, I want to thank You so much for this wonderful young man that I want to call my son. He has taught this old lady the love of kids and grandkids. I just want to pray, Lord God, for his protection and that he would be used by You to do a great work. I pray that You would send a legion of angels to protect and take charge over his family that they could fulfill the work You have for them. I just pray, Father, if I don't see them on this side of heaven, that You would keep them in Your care until I can make it up there. I love them very much, Father, and my heart is going to hurt without them, but I offer them to You, Father. Thank You for bringing them into my life! It's in Your son's name I pray and Amen!"

I get up and embrace Mary. We both cry and hold each other. She looks up at me with tears in her eyes and says, "You get out there, and you fight! You shake up the foundation of hell and give Satan something to fear. Hold the course and fight for everything you have. I'm so proud of you, son, and I know I will see you again one day soon."

She lets go of my face and walks away. I continue crying and feeling the great loss that I feel in my heart for not seeing her every day for however long I will be gone. I will do whatever I have to do to make her proud of me and to honor God with the sacrifices I'm making and the lives I'm going to be touching.

CHAPTER 14

I WAKE UP EARLY this morning. My goal is to slip out quietly so as to not make a big fuss of me leaving. I wake up Jacob and Jessica and get them moving. We already have everything packed, so it's just a matter of gathering it up and going. I look over where Mary usually sits, and I don't see her there. I can imagine she doesn't want things to be any more difficult than they already are. We make our way outside and look around to make sure the coast is clear. It looks like the sun has not yet peaked the horizon, but there is some light in the sky. We are now leaving the safety of our headquarters and venturing out into the unknown with purpose but no protection other than God. If this doesn't test a person's faith, I don't know what will.

We make our way to a road, and we're just trusting that God will get us where He wants us to go. As we sit there and wait for a ride to our next destination, I pray that it won't take too long. I really don't want to attract the attention of law enforcement. I opted to have no identification; I'm not safe with it anyway. My name is linked to a warrant for my capture and death, so I'm better off without it.

We see a semitruck making its way up the road. I quickly throw my thumb out, and he pulls over and picks us up. We climb into the truck, and the driver asks us where we're headed. I tell him, "Wherever you're headed, that's where we'll go." He smiles and then takes off. I'm really hoping he's okay and not some sort of weirdo.

We are driving along, and Jacob and Jessica are in the bunk and lying down, taking a nap. The driver looks over at me and says, "Hey, I'm Chad. What's your name?"

I reply, "I'm John. I really appreciate you picking us up."

He looks back at Jacob and Jessica and then back at me and asks, "So what's your story? Are you guys running from somewhere or running to somewhere?" I smile and say, "Well, a little of both really. We are on a mission, and we're just waiting on directions."

Chad responds, "I see. Directions from whom?"

I'm not smiling anymore, and I don't think I can tell him without causing myself some problems. I reply, "It's complicated, but we'll figure it out."

Chad looks at me and says, "You know, John, there are more of us out here than you realize. Also, this law might be an infringement, and it might be wrong all around, but there are many of us fighting out here for what's right. Just like prohibition, we're waiting for the day that the government will see what kind of mistake they made and will correct this decision."

I'm really shocked that Chad even knows anything about what I'm doing and why I didn't want to talk. I mention, "You know, you're pretty smart for a truck driver."

He laughs, nods, and says, "Well, I don't know whether I should be offended or feel complimented. I'm going to take it as a compliment."

I laugh and then reply, "Well, I think you should take that as a compliment. I don't know how you could know what we're doing, but we are doing God's work."

We continue on talking for hours as we drove for miles and miles. Chad talks to me about things, and boy, can this guy talk. He knows so much about quite a few things. I feel rejuvenated and thrilled that there are still people in this country who are fighting for our rights.

Chad asks me, "So are you married?"

I look at Chad, and I can feel the tears welling up. I respond, "I was, and my wife was killed in Philadelphia for her faith in God. I miss her so much, but I'm going out here, and I'm doing whatever I can to ensure people know about Jesus Christ, and I believe that will ensure she didn't die in vain, but rather, there is purpose. I plan on seeing her again someday."

He looks at me and nods. "I'm sorry for your loss. I can't imagine what that was like, but I'm going to be praying for you and your family. I know God is going to do some amazing things in your life."

The sun has finally come up, and I can see that traffic is picking up. I notice some signs, and it looks like we're getting into Pittsburgh. I look at Chad and ask, "Are you planning on stopping in Pittsburgh, by any chance?"

Chad says, "Yeah, I was actually planning on stopping and getting fuel. Is this where you would like me to drop you and your family off?"

I look at him and say, "Yes, I believe this is where we're getting off."

We pull into the truck stop, and he pulls up to the fuel island. I shake Jacob and Jessica and get them woke up. As we step down out of the truck, Chad comes around our side to unscrew his fuel cap, and he says, "Here, I want you guys to have this." As I look down, he is holding some money rolled up with a rubber band around it. Chad says, "I was saving this for my vacation to Aruba, but I think your mission is more important."

I can't do this to him. I respond, "Chad, we can't do that to you. We have a few bucks. We'll be okay."

"If you don't take this, you're going to hurt my feelings and keep me from a blessing," Chad rebuttals.

I look down at the money, and I know we're going to need it. I take the money and say, "Thank you so much for the ride and for helping us. You have no idea what this means to us."

Chad replies, "I do know what it means, and it's truly my pleasure." Chad extends his hand to shake, and I use his hand to pull him in for a hug.

I say to Chad, "God bless you, brother. I pray God's richest blessings on your life."

We turn and walk away, and I put the roll of cash in my pocket. As we start walking through town, I notice it isn't in as bad of shape as Philly, but you can definitely see there is still some opposition here once upon a time.

I begin to pray. "Father, we're here. Please point us in the right direction. Show us where we need to go and who we need to talk to about getting this software off the ground here in Pittsburgh. I pray You continue to protect us, Father. Keep us mindful of You and help us to keep You where You belong in our lives. We love You, Father, and thank You for Your countless blessings. I offer this prayer up to You in Your son's name, Jesus Christ. Amen."

It looks like we are approaching the rough side of town. There are lots of abandoned buildings and people living on the street. I notice a hotel up ahead and think this can be a good place to stop. It's out of the way, and I don't imagine law enforcement will be looking for anybody like me there.

I walk into the hotel, and the guy at the check-in counter was a rough-looking character. I wonder if he is related to the woman whom I encountered in Philly with the mole in her mouth. This guy has one in his mouth too, and he smells to high heaven. Whoa! I ask him, "Good afternoon. Do you have vacancy here? If so, do you offer a weekly rate?"

He leans forward, burps up his lunch, and then says, "We have a few rooms open. The weekly rate is $100."

So I respond, "Okay, let me see how much I have." I turn around and pull the roll of cash out of my pocket. As I unroll it, I see it's $100 on the outside of the roll. I flattened the money out and started counting it. Wow, it's about $800! Thank the Lord for Chad! He really bailed us out on this one. I slap my $100 on the counter and tell the front desk guy to set us up for a week. He quickly gets us checked in and gives us the key to the room.

We walk into the room, and it's not much to look at. There are two beds, and it looks like it was maybe new in 1955. I look at Jacob and Jessica and say, "God is taking care of us. At least we have a roof over our head and a warm bed to sleep in, even if we have to share the room with other little critters."

I sit those two down on the bed and ask them, "I know you two know what we're doing, but do you understand the importance of what I'm doing?"

Jacob responds, "I think making sure people know how to reach God, right?"

I smile and nod in affirmation. Jessica responds, "I agree. I looked at the software in the truck when your phone was charging, and I think you did such an amazing job. I'm so proud that we're the ones who are making this possible."

I say, "I'm so proud of the two of you. You have shown me how blessed I am, and I couldn't be more proud and love you more. It's important for you to know that I will have to go out and make a contact to see where the underground church is here. It's going to be dangerous, but I believe God will guide me. Here is the cash. If I'm not back within three days, take the cash and go get a bus ticket back to Philly. I know Mary will take care of you, and I want you two safe. Do you understand me?" They both nod in agreement. I say, "I'm going to go out now. I love you two very much. Stay strong and pray for your dad. I'm going to need it."

I walk out the door and begin making my way through the copious number of transients lying around. I know every area is going to be different, and nobody said this was going to be easy. In fact, I would even say that God made it clear this would be tough. So far, I would be inclined to agree with that.

As I continue walking around downtown and other side streets, I see no evidence of an underground church anywhere. No symbols, nothing. I see a café on the corner and decide to go in and drink a little coffee. As I sit there drinking my coffee, I begin to pray. "Father, this place is tough. There is no doubt that You gave me direction in Philly when I was looking for your direction. I'm praying now for direction, Father. I'm praying that You will either put me in somebody's path or put them in my path. I thank You, Father!"

As I start sipping my coffee, somebody is sitting two stools down from where I am sitting. He scoots over to the one next to me and says, "Hey, are you from around here?"

I reply, "No, I'm not. I'm just looking for something."

He goes on to drinking his coffee. He looks at me again and says, "Can I ask you a question?" I nod with affirmation. He says, "If I ask you, none are good, no not one, what would you say to me?"

With my eyebrows furled, I take the leap of faith and say, "I would say, except your Father in heaven."

He smiles and then hands me a card. It looks like a small business card. There is nothing on it except an address. He says to me, "Tell no one we have spoken and share this information with nobody. Meet me here at this address at midnight. At that time, I will share some things with you that will help you. I look forward to seeing you there."

As quickly as he finishes speaking, he is out the door. I smile and look up toward heaven and say, "Thank you, Father. Please keep me safe tonight."

CHAPTER 15

I WALK OUT OF the diner and pull the address up on my phone. I'm about eight blocks from this location on the card. I have plenty of time to get there, so I start making the journey to the address. As I walk that way, I notice the area continues to get uglier and more run-down. There are about a million things going through my mind, though, as I continue toward the address. What is it he is going to talk to me about? Is he even a Christian? Are they going to hurt me and take my things? I literally have no idea, and I would be lying if I said I wasn't nervous. Trusting God takes so much patience and faith sometimes it's hard to put myself out there. He's the kicker. I know this is what it's going to be like in every town that I go in. Nobody will know me, and I won't know them. I have to weed out the Christians in every town so I can show them this software. Therein lies the challenge and danger.

I'm about a block from the address, and things around here are pretty scary-looking. There are very few streetlights that even work, and the ones that do work aren't working very well. So naturally, it's difficult to see anything around here. I peer around the corner where the address is, and I don't see anybody. I know I'm a little bit early, but I was still hoping I would be able to get a good look at the people before I committed to trusting them. I decide to sit next to the dumpster in this alley and wait until closer to time to see if I can see anybody. Every little sound sets me on edge. Sometimes I think I hear something, and I move slowly and try and look as sharply as I can. This is tormenting for sure.

Finally, it's about ten minutes before midnight, and I still see nobody. Now I'm thinking either this guy was wasting my time or they lie in wait, ready to ambush me. My only recourse is to go and trust God. I begin to pray. "Father, I'm terrified! I have a feeling this is You and You're involved somehow, but this taking leaps of faith stuff is hard to do. I pray that You keep me in Your care, Father, to whatever end I face. Father, keep my kids in Your care. I pray that Your will prevails above all else. In Jesus's name, I pray. Amen."

I come out from behind the dumpster and begin to make my way over to the other corner where I'm supposed to be. As I approach, I believe I can hear some murmuring or whispers.

I arrive at the spot and just lean up against the wall in waiting. Out of the blue and out of nowhere, a group of guys approach me from all sides. This is a very rough bunch, and they look like gang members. I'm in deep trouble! As they are upon me now, one of the guys pulls a knife and says, "Put this bag over your head. If you know what's good for you, you won't make a noise, and you will comply." What else am I going to do but comply? I slowly put the bag over my head, and of course, I shake my head like I knew I shouldn't have come here. I feel two of the men grab my arms and begin to escort me. After walking for about ten minutes or what seems like a half an hour, we go into a place that smells bad, and I can hear more people talking now than before. As we continue in, I can hear a door open and then close behind me. They sit me down on a chair and say nothing to me.

Somebody behind me pulls the hood off, and there is a guy standing before me. He looks rough and not very friendly. He asks, "Why are you here?"

I answer the only way that I can. "I was given a card by the guy at the café, and he told me to come to the address at midnight. I have done that, but I have done nothing else."

He gets forceful and asks, "Who did you tell about coming here? Don't lie to me because we already know!"

I begin to look around as though I have no idea what in the world he is talking about. I reply, "I didn't talk to anybody! I don't know anybody in this area!"

He asks me, "Where are you from?"

I tell him, "I am coming from Philadelphia. I'm on a mission of great importance. I don't know what you guys are doing or what your goal is, but God has sent me out. If you hate God, I guess you'll have to kill me. My work ends when I die."

The guy standing in front of me looks behind me and motions to come to him. I hear some footsteps behind me and can tell they are coming around me. As I can now see the figure that was walking up from behind me, he leans down to my face and says, "What kind of a mission are you on? Any lies or funny business and it will be dealt with harshly and swiftly."

I tell them, "I'm revolutionizing the way Christians meet and making it more easily accessible for them all. I cannot tell you any more than that because I don't know you!"

The man stands there and studies me for a few moments and then responds, "So what you're telling me is you're a Christian and you're willing to die for your faith and you refuse to tell me anything else? You also know that I can kill you right now and nobody would ever know it was me?"

I respond accordingly, "Yes, I am a Christian. Yes, I'm willing to die right now, and if you wish to kill me, get on with it."

Now I don't know about you, but I have played some poker in my day. I'm telling you right now, I don't want to die, but I'm willing to die if need be. I put on my best poker face and just held it there.

He leans back out away from me and says, "My name is Darin. I represent this group of people. I'm the leader, if you will. We are all Christians, and we are also willing to die for our faith. Isn't it amazing what a person finds out about themselves when their faith is put to the test?"

Oh my goodness! I can actually breathe now. I look at Darin and respond, "Whoa, I was really hoping you didn't kill me. In fact, I don't think I'll ever be able to use these shorts again."

Darin pulls me up and says, "We're all on the same team. Tell me, what do you have that will revolutionize the way we meet?"

I begin to show him the software and how it works. He is absolutely floored and totally shocked by what I'm showing him. When I run through the software with him, he absolutely agrees that it will change the way they meet. I ask Darin, "So how do you meet now?"

Darin tells me, "We use the city map from the tourism office. We then just use the sections that are blocked off in the map. It's pretty unreliable because each square represents about eight square blocks. So unless you know the area pretty good, you'll never find where we meet."

I mention to him, "Yes, and this software utilizes satellite software to an accuracy of fifteen feet of where the location is. Tell me, how many groups do you think there are in this area alone?"

Darin sits and ponders for a moment. "Well, I would say there are at least fifteen groups that I know of but probably more."

I ask Darin, "Wouldn't it be nice if you all could meet at any location in town? Wouldn't it be nice to offer access to your new people that would allow them to know all of the locations in town? If the area ever becomes compromised, change the password, and nobody has unauthorized access again. It's not completely 100 percent, but we have done just about everything that we can do to ensure the safety of the Christians." I begin to explain the security of the software and the hierarchy of the software. I ask Darin if I can set him up as the governor of the area, and he excitedly agrees to do it.

I get his information and quickly make a phone call to our headquarters. When I call, I hear Bob on the other end. "Hello, how can I help you?" I figured this would be a good time to test Bob on his phone skills.

I quickly respond, "Yeah, I want to know what you all do?"

Bob responds with "Well, we are in the business of helping others. However, we don't volunteer our help. We help when you're selected."

I reply, "Bob, it's John! How you doing, brother?"

Bob laughs and lights up. "JOHN! How are you doing out there?"

I enthusiastically reply, "I'm doing pretty good now. Hey, listen, I have Darin here, and I want you to set him up as the governor of this area. I gave you the access you need to do this. I'm going to let you talk to him so you can get all the information you need from him. I appreciate you, Bob!"

I hand off the phone to Darin, and they begin to talk and do their thing. As the conversation draws to a close, Bob wishes Darin a blessed night and God's richest blessings.

I look at Darin and say, "Okay, Darin, keep recruiting however you see fit. However, send your guys out to talk to the other groups in town that they could be set up as editors, and this will become a thriving and successful area for Christians. God bless you and your work here!"

I shake Darin's hand and begin my long journey back to the hotel room. This was a great day, and I'm excited to see what tomorrow will bring.

CHAPTER 16

I AM MAKING MY way back to the hotel. I couldn't be happier that our first town is a success. I'm not ignorant enough to believe it's going to be easy everywhere we go, not that this was easy.

I get back to the hotel, and Jacob and Jessica are so thrilled to see me. They both run to me and hug me as hard as they can. Jacob says, "I'm so glad we didn't have to leave without you and that you're okay. I didn't really want to go, and this place scares me."

I look at Jacob and smile and then say, "Well, I'm here, and I'm very happy to see you both. We have a long road ahead of us, but I believe if we stick together, we will get through this. This is dangerous, and I don't want to be anywhere without my kids. I love you two very much!"

As we start bedding down for the night, I notice Jessica has a bit of a cough. I guess anything is possible, but it can just be a summer cold. I ask Jessica, "Are you doing okay, honey?"

She responds, "I'm okay. I've just been coughing, and my head hurts."

I feel her forehead, and she seems a bit warm. I go down to the front desk and ask for some Tylenol. Of course, they have some, and I take it back to the room. I give Jessica the Tylenol, and off to sleep we go.

Early the next morning, we begin to make our way out wherever the road takes us. So once again, we begin to head West. We find the ride that God sends us, and off we go.

Over the next couple of days, we manage to get Columbus, Ohio, signed up on the software as well as Cincinnati and Indianapolis. We are growing by leaps and bounds! Among the five cities that we have signed up in the last couple of days, we have somewhere in the neighborhood of two hundred groups signed up from these cities. I just couldn't be more thrilled.

We manage to make it in to St. Louis, and we find us a cheap place to stay there. We still have a wad of the trucker money, but the groups in Columbus and Indianapolis also gave us some money to run on. So we're actually doing pretty good with what we have. However, the issues that Jessica is having are getting even worse. She is now consistently running a fever, headaches, and she is having difficulty breathing. I guess this could still be the cold bug or maybe even flu, so I make the decision to take her to the hospital to make sure she gets the care she needs. I don't make this decision lightly. After all, anytime we have to give information about ourselves, we risk everything.

We get to the hospital, and we get her in the emergency room. They feel her, and she is very hot. They check her temperature, and it's currently 103.2 degrees Fahrenheit. The doctor comes in and looks over the symptoms and asks, "How long has she been like this?"

I reply, "Well, I would say two or three days now. I just thought it might be the cold or flu, but it doesn't seem to be getting any better, and now she is having a hard time breathing."

The doctor draws some blood and orders X-rays of her lungs. We are at the emergency room for probably six hours, and it seems even longer. We are just waiting, and Jessica seems to be getting sicker, and now she's feeling very nauseous. The nurses keep coming in to check on her and giving her more medications to help with the symptoms.

After a total of eight hours, the doctor comes in and says, "Okay, I have some bad news. This isn't the cold or flu virus. It's much worse. Most people actually confuse the symptoms with that of a cold or flu. You see here, between the red spots on various parts of her body and the X-rays, we were thinking she might have contracted the hantavirus. However, the blood results are conclusive. She does have the hantavirus. Because it is a virus, there is no cure. We just have to let it run its course. We currently have her on oxygen to help with the respiratory distress, but outside of that, there isn't a lot we can do but deal with the symptoms. We are going to have to admit her, and we're going to have to send her right up to intensive care. Tell me, have you lived in any situations where there could have been mice or a dirty living environment?"

Right away, I knew where he was going with this. I respond, "Well, things have been a little rough for us and maybe not so favorable, but yes, there could have been mice."

The doctor responds, "I would like to get blood work of you and your son to ensure you're not carrying the virus as well. Would that be okay? It isn't contagious, but if you have come into contact with the same elements that Jessica has come into contact with, you could be infected too. The earlier we can begin to treat it, the better the chances of beating it."

"Wait a second, are you telling me that Jessica might not be able to beat this?" I mutter.

The doctor replies, "I'm sorry, but if we had gotten to her sooner, she wouldn't be this bad off. I would say the prognosis isn't good. The chances of her making it the next couple of days are less than 10 percent. I'm truly sorry. Now let's get that blood work to ensure you two are okay."

The nurse comes in and takes our blood and then sends them to the lab. I ask the nurse, "How long before we'll know about my son and me?"

The nurse replies, "We should know within an hour or two."

My heart begins beating fast, and I can feel my chest tighten. I can't lose my daughter! I've lost too much already, and I need my kids. As I sit here rationalizing, I can feel the tears streaming down my face. There is nothing worse than watching your daughter fight for her life, and you're helpless to do anything for her. I'm devastated, and I don't know what to do about it. I grab Jacob, and I just hold him. I smell his hair and kiss his cheek, and as I sit there holding him, I begin to pray, "Father, I'm desperate here. We're out here doing Your work and Your will. The doctor is telling me that my daughter is going to potentially die, and I just can't deal with that. Father, I need my kids! I need them with me. It was bad enough that I had to lose Layna. I'm desperate here, Father. I need You now. Please." I just can't help but cry. It hurts in my heart, stomach, chest, everywhere!

The nurse comes back in the room after about an hour and says, "You and your son are clear. Neither one of you are carrying the virus." Praise God, but my daughter is, and she's not getting any better. The nurse comes back in and tells me, "There will be a lady in here shortly to get your name and information. It shouldn't take her too long."

I just need to be alone for a few minutes. So I ask Jacob to stay put, and I will be right back. I sit in the bathroom and break down. I feel like God isn't hearing me. Jessica is getting no better, and she's struggling more now than she was even this morning. I need to be strong for Jacob right now. So I get back up and head back to the room.

When I get back in there, the registration lady is already in there. The registration lady says, "Okay, Mr. Burton, your son has already filled me in on the small details, but I will need your insurance information. Also, are you guys just visiting in this area? I notice you're from out of town." I know my eyes had to have been huge. Jacob gave the registration lady our personal information, not knowing that he was going to lead law enforcement right to us.

I couldn't produce a license and any insurance card, so the registration lady says, "Okay, I will take what information I have for now. I'll be right back." I see her go to the nurse's station. She gets on the phone, and I can see her talking to somebody on the phone and then looking back at me several times. All I can hear is police and warrant.

We are in so much trouble. We can't stay here, or we will surely die. I walk up to Jessica while she was lying in her bed and whisper to her, "Honey, I think the cops are coming here to get us. If we stay here, we will all die, including you. We have to leave here." She musters what little strength she has and says yes.

We wait for our opening to leave, and we take it. We get about two blocks from the hospital, and I can hear sirens, and I begin to see the cars approaching the hospital. We walk as far as we can and stay in this little hotel about eight blocks from the hospital. We get checked in, and I get the kids up to the room. I put Jessica on the bed and just look at her and touch her hand.

I sit there holding my daughter's hand and watching her. I remember back to when she was just a little girl. When she was first born, I felt the greatest pride I have ever known. To know that this little girl was a great gift and I was privileged to get to be her daddy. I can feel the tears rolling down my cheek as I feel completely defeated and heartbroken. Parts of me feel like she is fighting a losing battle, and I'm helpless to do anything.

I begin to pray. "Father, I need Your power and Your presence right now. Please help to heal her, Father. I just don't think I have the strength to do this right now. Amen." I lay my head on her legs and wait. Wait for what? I don't know.

CHAPTER 17

"DADDY, WAKE UP." I hear in this sweet little voice.

My eyes slowly open, and I realize I'm not in the hotel room anymore. I ask, "Where are we? How did we get here?" Wait! It's Jessica! I ask, "How are you feeling? I was so worried about you!"

Jessica replies, "Daddy, I don't have a lot of time."

"You don't have a lot of time? Honey, we have all the time in the world," I remark.

Jessica says, "Daddy, I just want you to know how proud of you I am. I think you're a remarkable father, and you did a great job of raising Jacob and I. You have gone through some really horrible things, and you have managed to keep things together for us. I want you to keep doing what you're doing because without this help that you're giving people, they have very little chance of doing what they need to do."

I'm a bit confused and respond accordingly, "Jessica, why are you telling me all of this? You make it sound like you're leaving me."

Jessica replies, "Mom is waiting for me, Dad. Please don't blame yourself. You have no reason to. I love you very much, and I'll see you soon, but I have to go."

Panic and worry set in, and I become frantic. I can see her walking away, and I'm helpless to move. "Wait, Jessica, where are you going? Please don't leave me!"

I wake up with tears running down my cheeks as my head is lying on the bed where I went to sleep. As I look up, I can see that my baby girl isn't breathing any longer. I hold her and pull her close to my chest and cry out, "Father, why? Why couldn't You have spared her for me? I love her so much!"

I hold her in my arms and just feel her hair against my arm, and I think of times gone by that I would bounce her on my knee or swing her through the air as she was flying. The once beautiful and vibrant daughter of mine is gone. I will never see her again this side of heaven.

Jacob wakes up and sees my crying, and he walks up to me and says, "Daddy, what's wrong?"

I reply, "She went to heaven to be with Mommy, buddy. I'm so sorry!" I pull him in close to me and let him cry too.

My chest hurts so badly. I don't know how a person can be put through so much and survive. I'm exhausted, and my heart feels like it's in a million pieces. What do I do now? Maybe I should have left her in Philly with people I trusted. Maybe I should have taken her to a doctor sooner.

Then my mind goes back to the dream that I had. It seemed so real. Maybe that was God granting her the opportunity to talk to me one last time. I know she said it wasn't my fault, but it feels like my fault. She believes in me, and so does Jacob. I can't let my family down.

After what seems like an eternity of crying and remembering, I decide we need to get moving. I lay Jessica down on the bed, and I kiss her cheek and then whisper in her ear, "I'll see you soon, sweetheart."

Jacob and I get back on the road again. We hitch a ride with a little family that is traveling to California for their vacation. They are a quiet bunch and don't really say too much to us. As they let us out in Kansas City, I notice the husband hands me a little cash and tells me good luck. I smile and thank him and then move on out.

It is pretty much the same routine everywhere we go, but I don't feel like I should leave Jacob in the hotel rooms by himself anymore. Maybe people won't suspect me of anything if I'm with a child. Maybe it makes me look more vulnerable.

So we get to the hotel, and we decide to lie down and take a nap. As we lie there listening to a quiet room, I hear Jacob ask, "Dad, did you ever think things were going to turn out like this?"

I reply, "Not at all like this, son. I never would have guessed this was how things were going to turn out."

Jacob asks, "We have lost so much. Why do you think God is allowing this to happen to us? Do you think we are going to die too?"

I sit up in bed and turn on the light and respond, "Listen, buddy, I don't know what God has in store for us. One thing I do know, if we continue to do God's work, no matter what happens to us, we will get to see Mommy and

Jessica again. I'm scared too, but sometimes bad things happen to good people. We just have to trust God that He knows what He's doing."

Jacob nods and says, "Yeah, I miss seeing Mom's face, and I miss hearing her voice."

I smile and nod. "Yeah, me too, buddy . . . me too."

I can't help but feel the pain in my chest. Losing Jessica is like losing Layna all over again. It just reopens the injury and makes it hurt all over again. I lie there in bed staring at the ceiling but seeing Jessica in my head. The dream that I had means so much more to me now than it did at the time. I didn't know that was the last time I was going to see my little girl alive.

I lie there in bed and think about that morning we were at home, and we were all having a good morning.

I remember I am walking through this mud, and it is up to my waist. It is so thick that I can hardly move. All around me, there are people dying and being tortured. I can hear crying and wailing. Behind me, I can see this man dressed in a black robe. The robe covers him completely, and the hood goes down over his face. He is walking on top of the mud and isn't inhibited like I am. No matter how fast I try pushing through the mud, it seems like he just continues gaining on me.

I look forward, and I see Layna standing across this great chasm. She's holding a small child, the same one whom I had seen before. From behind Layna, I can see Jessica, and Layna puts her arm around Jessica and pulls her in close. They are all three smiling at me, and Layna says, "We love you, John. Stay strong, and we'll see you soon."

As I take my eyes off Layna, I look behind me, and the man in black is within arm's reach of me. Just before he touches me, I wake up.

I sit up in bed and begin to cry and pray, "Father, I miss my family so much. I need Your strength, Father. I'm trying to stay strong, but I'm feeling so weak right now. Help me to overcome this pain so that I can continue the journey You have placed before me. To whatever end I might meet, Father, I do this all for You! Amen."

Later on that evening, I look at Jacob and tell him, "Okay, no more sitting here alone in the room. I need you to know that I love you very much, and if we are going to die, we're going to do it together. Okay?"

Jacob looks at me with a little soldier face and says, "Okay, Dad! Together!"

It's about 7:30 p.m., and we set off to figure out what we can do in this area. It's a pretty good-sized town, so naturally, we have a long night ahead of us. We continue down alleys and backstreets to no avail. We are just looking for anything and everything that may give us a clue as to what Christians there may be.

As we turn the corner, we see a military street patrol making their way toward us. As they are walking along, they are scanning people's faces, and some of them are getting arrested, and some of them are being pushed back down on to the street.

I stand there looking too long because they spot me and yell out, "Hey, you! Get over here!" I grab Jacob by the hand, and we begin to run. Naturally, he doesn't run nearly as fast as me, but I don't think we're going to outrun them. We're going to have to try to outsmart them. We manage to find a building with a side door that is open. We run in and close the door. I can hear them outside looking for us, but I think we lost them.

I decide to hunker down for a while to wait them out. I pull my phone out, and I call Bob. Bob picks up the phone and says, "Hi, how may I help you?"

I reply, "Hey, Bob, it's me, John."

Bob replies, "John! How are things going out there?"

I reply, "Well, not so great. We're hiding in a building right now to avoid being captured. We also lost Jessica to a virus in St. Louis. Could you make sure to let Mary know about that, please?"

There is a pause on the phone, and Bob replies, "I'm so sorry, John! You have lost so much, and I'm sorry you have to do this. Just know I'm here if you ever need anything, and I will definitely let Mary know as well. I have some good news if you could use some of that."

I respond, "At this point, I'll take any good news."

Bob excitedly replies, "Well, I sent out messages to all of our groups that are currently signed up, and I basically had them do what you're doing. I assumed you were headed West, so I had them send out groups going East, South, and North of us here to get people signed up. Well, I'm happy to say we have another thirteen cities signed up and more than six hundred groups signed up as well. This is growing into something I never even imagined. In fact, we had to bring on more people here at the headquarters to help field phone calls because we couldn't keep up anymore. Isn't that great news?"

I am so beyond thrilled that this is taking off. I tell Bob, "Wow, God really is doing an awesome thing here! I can't believe how quickly this is growing, and I'm so glad that I have you there helping me with this. I knew you were the right man for the job, and I couldn't be more proud of your progress. Keep up the good work and keep us lifted up in prayer. I'm going to get off of here, but I wanted to keep you updated."

Bob replies, "Thanks, John. You guys are doing great. Let us know if you need anything. We pray for you every day, and we will continue doing that until God calls us home."

As Bob and I hung up the phone, I really feel a renewed strength. God is really doing an amazing thing here, and it's because I was yielded to the calling that He has for me. As I begin to get up to see if the coast is clear, I hear something behind me, and I turn to look.

CHAPTER 18

I SEE A FEW silhouettes standing behind me. I hear, "Get up!" I slowly stand. I don't want to give them any reason to hurt me or Jacob. One of the guys approaches me, and as he gets closer, I can make out his face a little bit. He asks, "What are you doing here?"

I respond quietly, "I'm just hiding from the soldiers that were chasing us."

He asks, "Why were they chasing you? What have you done wrong?"

Truthfully, I am thinking it is another group of Christians who are weighing me to determine if I'm genuine. So I respond accordingly, "I'm a Christian, and they are trying to kill my son and me."

The guy stands there for a minute and then, all of a sudden, spits in my face. He grits his teeth and snarls his face and says, "It's because of worthless people like you we are all living in a war zone. I hate every last one of you. I'm going to turn you in and collect the bounty. I have to wait until morning because these morons outside will take you, and I won't see a penny. So I will be escorting you to the courthouse tomorrow myself!"

I really can't believe how this is working out. He grabs us and ties our hands behind our backs. He then escorts us to his little hideout. As I look around, they don't live a whole lot differently than we did at the headquarters. He says, "Look around! This is what you did to us . . . you and your people!"

What can I say? There really isn't anything I can say that he will believe. I respond, "Don't you think Christians have a right to believe and worship the god they choose? Why do you think it's right that we are told we cannot worship the god we choose? It was our constitutional right, and then they just took it from us, and not only that, we had to pretend like we never believed in anything, or we would die. You think that we are foolish idiots for fighting for what we believe in?"

He looks at me and smiles. "That's why we're fighting you and ridding the world of you, and then we can get back to a normal life!"

Like I said, it doesn't matter what I say; we are wrong. Jacob and I just sit there, and Jacob looks up at me and says, "Dad, do you think we're going to die?"

I reply, "They aren't going to kill us here. We are more valuable to them alive. However, if he delivers us to the court tomorrow, we will definitely be put to death." I can see the worry in Jacob's face, and my heart hurts for him, but I feel helpless to do anything to comfort him. "Listen, buddy, this is the plan that God has laid out for us. I can't promise nothing bad is going to happen to us. But I can promise that if we trust in God, we'll be with our family very soon." I try and console him.

Jacob asks, "Dad, how do I know if I trust God enough to make it to heaven?"

I smile and respond, "Do you believe in Jesus Christ and love Him?" He nods yes. I ask, "Do you try and live for Him to the best of your ability?" He nods yes. I remark, "Then you trust Him enough to make it to heaven. God doesn't expect us to be perfect, but He expects us to be obedient and work toward righteousness. Hang in there, buddy. One way or another, we are going to be in heaven soon."

As the sun sets, my mind goes back to Layna and Jessica. I miss them like flower misses the face of the sun. My heart aches for their touch and their voice. My thoughts help me soak in as much of my little boy as I can. One day I might have to find out what it's like to live without my little boy. I wait for that day but not with anticipation but with much anxiety. I would prefer to go together. As we lie there tied up, I feel myself drifting off to sleep.

I am walking through the mud again. This time it is a little different; it isn't up to my waist, but it is up to my chest. I remember having to try even harder to get through the mud and is moving even slower than I was before. When I look around, there are still people all around me dying, and I can't save them; I can hardly save myself. I maneuver myself to look behind me with great difficulty, and the man in black is behind me again. He is once again walking on top of the mud. Just like before, he is gaining on me with no effort, and I'm expending all this energy just to move.

Just like before, I look forward, and I see Layna standing across this great chasm. She's holding a small child, the same one whom I had seen before. From behind Layna, I can see Jessica, and Layna puts her arm around Jessica and pulls her in close. They are all three smiling at me, and Layna says, "We love you, John. Stay strong, and we'll see you soon."

I smile when I see them, but my smile is quickly thwarted when I glance behind me, and the man in black is within arm's reach of me. He is a force that I can't beat, and I know it. I cry out, "Father, help me! The mud aims to drown me, and the man in black aims to kill me. Help me!"

Just then, I hear the voice of God say, "Son, the mud is your journey, and soon, the mud will overtake you but not until your work is done. I will not allow the man in black to harm you. He answers to Me . . . I am." I look behind me, and the man in black is drowning in the mud and no longer able to walk on top of it. I hear God say, "Arise and go your way."

Just then, I wake up. I look around, and everybody is sleeping, including Jacob. I notice my hands and feet aren't bound up any longer. The ropes that were used to tie us up are on me but loose enough for me to slip my hands out of the ropes. I turn around and undo Jacob's ropes as well. I put my hand over his mouth and wake him up. I then whisper in his ear, "Hey, our ropes are off. We're going to make a run for it. Be very quiet. We can't afford to wake them up."

We begin to walk out very slowly. We make our way outside, but we're in some kind of a compound. There is a pretty sizable perimeter fence around where we are. I notice there are some people standing guard at various spots around the property. My goal is to find an easy way out and then go. The bad part about it is we are broke again. These people took all the money we had been given. We begin walking toward a part of the fence that is slightly damaged. I think we might be able to slip out there.

We get up to the fence, and we begin to work our way out of the fence. I make it out successfully, so I lift the fence a bit to help Jacob out. Just then, Jacob loses his balance and falls into the fence. It all happens in slow motion, and as soon as he hits the fence, it sends a rippling shock wave down the rest of the fence. Quickly, the people on guard look our direction and see us getting out of the fence.

Jacob quickly makes it out, and we start running. Again, Jacob isn't very fast, so our goal is to lose them with our brains and not our speed. I see a wooded area up ahead and figure I'll run in there and pull a Sherwood forest routine.

I look back, and all the lights come on, and the alarm sounds. If we don't lose them in the woods, we are goners for sure. We finally make it to the woods, and we hide behind a tree. I look at the compound, and I can see their gate opening up. There is a horde of people coming to find us. I look at Jacob and say, "Hey, buddy, we're going to have to run hard and fast for a long time to stay alive. Can you do it?" With a look of determination on his face, he nods in affirmation. I'm telling you, I don't think either one of us has ever run that fast. The bad part is, I am hearing vehicles behind us. There is no way we can outrun vehicles.

I begin to pray while running for my life. "Father, please help us get away. We have no hope of living if You don't help us. Please deliver us, Father." Within just a matter of ten or fifteen seconds after I prayed, I can hear a train up in the distance. We begin running toward the train. It can be our only option. As we make our way into the clearing, I can see the train moving but moving very slowly. I yell out to Jacob, "We need to get on that train!" As we get close, the train is moving faster. I'm also hearing them behind us, and they are nearly upon us. I look back, and I can see them piling out of the vehicles to try and get us. I look down at Jacob, and my heart starts hurting, I don't want to fail him. He needs me right now. Just then, I hear God say, "I will not allow the man in black to harm you. He answers to Me . . . I am."

I climb into the train and extend my hand out to grab Jacob. Just then, I start hearing them fire their weapons at us. I hear Jacob cry out, "Help me, Dad!" I grab his hand and pull him up into the train. I look back at the guys who had captured us, and they are all very upset and distraught. I'm sure they are wondering how in the world this all happened.

I sit and thank God for His mercy and for getting us out of there. I ask Jacob to come down and sit with me. I don't know where we're going, but it's not into captivity, so I'll take it.

Jacob sits and says, "Dad, I'm glad we made it. But my back is hurting. I think I hurt it when you pulled me into the train." I turn him around and look, and my worst fear is realized. He has been shot in the back. I have blood all over my hand and arm, and it's coming out of his back at a pretty good rate. I try to keep it held together, but I am so panicked. The train is moving too fast now to jump out, and I don't know when it's going to stop. So I take some plastic I see on one of the pallets and tie it around him to slow down the bleeding.

Jacob looks up at me and asks, "Dad, what's wrong with my back?"

I try and clean up my emotion off my face. "Well, buddy, it looks like you have an injury to your back, and I'm trying to make it better. Just hang in there. We might be stopping soon."

CHAPTER 19

AS I SIT there and wonder what is to become of my son as we are stuck in the train and he has a bullet in his back, I think about this journey. No matter how many times I think about it, it just sometimes seems like a really bad dream. I feel like I will wake up at any moment and praise the Lord for it being a bad dream. I just don't think that's going to happen.

I look down at my son, and I smile at him. He looks up at me and smiles back as his head lies on my leg. Then he says one of the funniest things I've heard him say for a while, "Daddy, I've sure had more fun . . . What do you say we do something else?"

I can't help but laugh. I reply, "You're right, buddy. Why don't we quit this game and do something else? How about a game of monopoly?"

His smile quickly vanishes, and he responds, "I promised Mom I would never play you again. You cheat."

With a look of astonishment, I say, "I never cheat. I just know how to stack the deck in my favor!"

Jacob says, "Yes, cheating."

I reply, "Okay, I guess you have a point, maybe it is."

Jacob asks, "Dad, why is it getting so cold outside?"

I reply, "Well, it's getting to be night, buddy. The sun's heat is gone." I know why he's getting cold, and it's not the sun; he's losing too much blood. I say, "Go ahead, buddy, close your eyes and rest. Just know how much I love you, and I will be here to protect you, okay?"

He looks up at me and smiles, "I know you will, Dad. I love you."

Jacob drifts off to sleep, and that gives me the opportunity to pray. I pray, "Father, please stop this train so my son can get the help he needs. I don't want to lose my little boy too. Father, I've lost so much, and I have shown You how much I love You and how much I'm doing for the kingdom. Could You spare him and take me? Please, Father . . . I'm begging! It's not my will, Father, but Your will."

I feel myself drift off to sleep. I remember seeing this great chasm, and I can see Layna, Jessica, and the little girl on the other side. They are smiling at me and waving. I can hear Layna calling my name. What I wouldn't give to embrace her just one more time! This time I'm in a field of wheat, and I'm naked. I turn around, and there is this huge combine harvesting the wheat, and it's toward me. I have never seen a combine so big. I look forward, and the wheat goes on for miles and miles. As I look to my sides, I see a vast number of people lined up watching me run and laughing at my nakedness. They keep chanting "Kill him," and from the looks of it, I'm not going to survive. Just before the combine pulls me into its teeth, I wake up.

I notice that the train is slowing down, and I can see a lot of lights. I try to stir Jacob to wake up, but he's very lethargic and is very sleepy. I pick him and sit at the edge of the door to jump off. We finally stop, and I jump off with Jacob in my arms. I almost wipe out, but I am able to stay on my feet.

As luck would have it, I hear an ambulance in the distance, and I can hear it getting closer. I begin jogging with Jacob in my arms to see if I can see which direction it's going. I finally see the ambulance peak over the hill, and I see it turning. It goes down about a block, and I hear the sirens turn off. I begin running as fast as I can toward where I last saw the ambulance, and there is a hospital there. I run into the emergency room and yell, "My son has been shot! Please help me!"

One of the doctors rushes over and asks, "How long has he been like this?"

I reply, "I'm not sure, a few hours maybe. We were stuck in a situation that we couldn't seek medical attention."

The doctor puts Jacob on the hospital bed and begins checking him over. He then spouts off a bunch of medical things that I don't know anything about. Next thing I know, there seems to be wires and hoses everywhere. Then about a half a dozen people rush in there, and they prepare to take him back to surgery.

I see Jacob's eyes open up a bit, and I say, "Hey, buddy, we're at the hospital. The doctors are going to try and fix you up, okay?" He can't muster the strength to say anything but shows me a little smile. I caress his face and say, "I sure love you, buddy. Thanks for being such a great sidekick!"

Before anything else is said, they whisk him off to surgery. One of the people in the ER take me to the waiting room to wait for Jacob. She shows me where I can get some coffee, and I can see the sympathy in her face, and she is helpless to do anything for me. I look at her and ask, "Ma'am, can you tell me where we are? I mean, what city this is?"

She smiles and says, "Sure. You're in Rockford, Illinois."

I can't believe it! How did we ride Kansas City to Rockford, Illinois, in a few hours? We couldn't have. That is a seven-hour drive in a car and probably takes longer than that on a train. I was out longer than I thought, and that means Jacob was injured and bleeding a lot longer than I thought. She turns around and makes her way back.

I start thinking that it would sure be nice to head back to Philadelphia and regroup and get a new game plan put together. As soon as Jacob is out of surgery and is able to travel, that's exactly what we're going to do.

I look at my phone as I sit and wait, and I log on to the app. I notice there are three groups right here in Rockford. Wow, this app is doing great! I was never even in Rockford, and yet we have 3 groups here. I zoom out to look at the whole world, and at that moment, I can feel the tears in my eyes. The tears quickly overtake my eyes, and they start streaming down my face. When I had spoken to Bob before, he had told me that we had a little over 600 groups signed up because everybody was spreading the word. What I didn't know is that those members were signing people up as well. The app now has more than 140,000 groups signed up. Not only are we in nearly every state now, but we are now in over fifty countries around the world as well.

How did this grow that fast? This is nearly impossible! It would take a miracle! At this moment, I realize this is the plan that God has for me. I knew this was the plan that God had for me, but I didn't really know that it was this big. I never knew how large this was going to be. I have a feeling it's going to continue to grow into this amazing thing. The flipside of this coin is this, there are that many people in the world so far who are willing to hazard death to worship with other believers. I'm astonished at how amazing my God is!

I navigate to another area of the app, and there is another area once clicked, it opens a Bible. Once the Bible opens, it shows me some of the features. If I need to close it quickly, just double tap the screen, and it automatically minimizes it so that it cannot be seen on the screen. There are some really awesome features that make this app just that much better. It looks like this Bible is available in over six hundred different languages. I cannot wait to talk to our people in Philadelphia and congratulate them on a job well done. I couldn't have left the "business" of the app to a better or more accomplished person.

So I have been sitting in this waiting room for nearly four hours. This can't be good. How could it take this long to get the bullet out of his back and get him into ICU? I just don't get it.

I walk up the nurses' station and ask, "Hi. I want to find out what happened to my son. He went back into surgery like four hours ago, and I haven't heard anything yet. What's going on?"

The lady at the desk looks up at me and says, "Sir, unfortunately, they don't tell us what they are doing and when they're going to be done. As soon as there is any news, I'm sure they will let you know."

I walk away from the nurses' station feeling even worse than I did before I walked up there. I sit there wringing my hands and watching the clock, and before I have a chance to get back up, I notice my son's doctor is walking toward me from down at the end of the hall. He walks in the waiting area and says, "Mr. Burton, let's talk."

CHAPTER 20

I SIT DOWN WITH the doctor, and he gets right to the point. "Look, Jacob lost nearly 50 percent of his blood, and the bullet punctured his liver. When we got him in here, he was already nearly dead. However, with a blood transfusion and some rest, I think he should make a full recovery," the doctor mentions. I'm so amazed. I honestly expected the worst. I have lost so much; I assumed I was going to lose my precious boy too.

I ask the doctor, "Doc, I can't even begin to express my gratitude. Thank you so much for saving my son's life! Can I go see him?"

He looks at me and says, "I'm sorry, I can't allow that. We feel as though he isn't being taken care of, and the Department of Child and Family Services has been contacted to assess whether or not he should remain with you. I'm sorry, we had no choice."

I know it sounds cynical, but I was waiting for the bad news. My life has been a series of bad events and loss. I sit there in the waiting room, and I begin to pray. "Father, I have put my life in Your hands. I've lost Layna, I've lost Jessica, and looks like I'm losing my son. Why does my life have to be a series of bad things and loss? Did I do something wrong? You spared my son's life, but now I'm being told that I could lose my son. I'm physically, mentally, and spiritually exhausted, Father. I don't know how much more of this I can take."

I sit there thinking about Jacob and how scared he must be knowing he can't see me. It is then that I hear God speak to me. "John, the elements that you have suffered are no different from thousands of people before you. Job suffered a horrible loss, and because you read about it and not see it, it doesn't have the same effect? My people all over the world have suffered great loss, you included. You suffer for a purpose. Stop focusing on the here and now. Look forward to the forevermore. You have accomplished a great work that I needed you to accomplish, but your work is not done. Go and get your son. It's time to go."

Go and get my son? I suppose I'm staging a coup to get my son and leave. I leave the waiting area and begin making my way down to my son's room. As I get closer, I see a hospital security guard standing at the entrance of my son's room. I dodge into a room and peer around the corner. He walks up to the nurses' station and begins chatting with a couple of the nurses who are standing there.

Just then, I hear over the intercom a Code Blue. Both the nurses rush off to help, I assume. As soon as they rush off, the security guard is given to complete curiosity at the Code Blue situation. I casually walk past the security guard and walk in the room. I see my son resting peacefully, and I walk up to him and slide my hand into his. I begin brushing his hair with my fingers and whisper into his ear, "Hey, buddy, you need to wake up. We have to go." After about three minutes of talking, he finally starts coming to.

"Dad," he mumbles.

I reply, "Hey, buddy, I'm here, and you're going to be okay. Listen, buddy, they are going to try and take you away from me. We have to go, or we may not get to see each other again." Jacob opens his eyes, and I can see he's just exhausted. "Come on, buddy, let's get you dressed," I whisper. I get Jacob dressed, and I look out the door. I notice the security guard is now moved around the counter and peering into the room that had the Code Blue. It's now or never. We slide out the door, but poor Jacob is barely holding it together. We make our way to the elevator and not one word from anybody about us. They probably have no clue that is Jacob since he just got shot.

The elevator door opens up, and standing before me is a lady with a briefcase. I look at the badge she is wearing, and it says Department of Child and Family Services. She glances at us and then gets out of the elevator. We are stone-cold. We don't let on like we are afraid or surprised. We make our way on the elevator and make our way down to the main floor. I can see the front door, and all we have to do is get outside and catch a cab.

Just then, over the intercom, I hear "Code Yellow." I have a good idea what a Code Blue means, but I don't know what a Code Yellow is. About that time, a couple of gentlemen from the reception station get up, and I hear one of them saying something about a missing patient. They rush over to the door and tell me that nobody is allowed to leave during a Code Yellow. I'm really terrified now as it won't take them long to figure out my son is the Code Yellow. I notice there is a cafeteria sign, and I begin to make my way down there. I go into the cafeteria, and I sit down. I don't know what to do. Where do I go?

I look over, and I see the kitchen. I grab Jacob, and we begin making our way into the kitchen. At the far end of the kitchen, I see an exit door. We continue our walk toward the door. Right before we get to the door, I hear a kitchen worker. "Sir, you aren't allowed to be back here."

I reply, "Oh, I'm sorry, I'll step out and go around." The kitchen worker nods and then continues on with what she was doing.

I open the door and walk outside. It's a fairly dirty alley, so I figure we'll be okay back here. I start walking opposite of the front of the hospital to get away from there as quickly as possible. What was I thinking? I can't grab a cab; I have no money. I look at my phone to get my bearings in town, and I see that we are about five blocks from the interstate. We make our way through downtown and find the interstate on-ramp that is going east. I stand there with a thumb out and hoping and praying somebody stops.

After about a twenty-minute wait, a guy who is in a semi stops and asks, "Hey, where are you guys headed?"

I jump on the side and tell him, "We're headed back to Philadelphia."

He replies, "Hop in. I'm headed to New York City. I can drop you off on the way."

Praise the Lord! We get up inside, and I ask him, "Would you mind if my son lies in the bunk? He's really tired?"

The trucker responds, "Not at all. It would probably work out better for seating anyway." So I lay Jacob in the bunk and buckle him in. We begin our journey back to Philly. The trucker says, "Hi, my name is Chris. What's your name?"

I respond, "Hi, Chris, my name is John."

The trucker asks, "So where are you guys from?"

I reply, "Well, we've been many places, but our home is in Philadelphia now. What about you?"

He looks at me and smiles. "This is my home. Since all of this stuff in this country has started, I have been living in my truck. It makes it easier for me to do the things I like to do. Let me ask you a question. You look like you have had a rough go of it. Have you placed your trust with Jesus Christ?"

I look at him, and I know what kind of a risk he is taking by even bringing up the name of Jesus Christ. I look at him and ask, "You do realize that even mentioning the name of Jesus is punishable by death, right?"

He nods yes and then says, "Yeah, I understand that. I guess I just thought it looked like you might need to know who Jesus is. So to me, it seems like it's worth the risk."

I smile at him and tell him, "I know Jesus Christ as my personal savior. I'm actually at the tail end of a mission that I had been working on."

The trucker smiles and says, "Well, I wondered about that. Can I ask you what mission you were on?"

I tell him, "Yes, I am the inventor and creator of a software used to connect Christians with other Christians. It's called Ma tovu ohalecha."

His eyes get really big, and he exclaims, "That's you!"

I ask him, "So you've heard of it, huh?"

He proclaims, "Of course! With me driving, it's great to know where I can go when I stop for the night. I love to fellowship with other believers. You know, in a way, we are getting more church now than we were before because of all of this. It used to be we would just go to church on Sundays, and sometimes if I was home, I would go Wednesdays. Now I can go nearly every day because of the software. It has literally brought me closer to Jesus! Thank you so much for creating this!"

I can't believe it! I'm sitting in a truck with a driver who is not only a Christian but is also using my software regularly to connect with other believers. That is unbelievable! I tell him, "I'm so happy that you're getting use out of the software. That's exactly why I created it."

I get in the app and take a look. I can't even believe how quickly it's growing. We now have about 162,000 groups. Wow! We also have nearly six million users. This software is growing to epic proportions. I guess this is why you don't put God in a box!

We chitchat for the remainder of the drive back to Philly. We talk about software and just life in general and spent time praying and citing scripture. What was to be a thirteen-hour drive from Rockford felt so much shorter because of this great guy whom I got to spend it with. It was so amazing to get to connect with another Christian. The time with him was much needed and so appreciated. God knew what I needed when I didn't.

We finally pull into Philadelphia, and it's been a long day. It's dark outside, but I tell Chris where he can go to get me close to the headquarters. I get up and walk to the bunk. I rest my hand on Jacob's head and say, "Hey, Jacob, we're home. Let's get inside so you can hit the bunk."

I look at Chris and smile. "Listen, brother, I'm so glad that God put me in your life! Look me up anytime you're in town again. I would love to meet with you again." He smiles and then shakes my hand and takes off to finish his journey.

Jacob and I start the walk down into the sewer to get to the headquarters. Whew, it really stinks in here tonight. Believe it or not, I actually missed the smell of the sewer. It means being with people that I have come to love and respect.

We walk into the headquarters to find that it's completely empty and trash everywhere. What in the world happened? Were they caught? What is to become of the people that I know? I find a corner of the headquarters with a mattress lying on the ground, and Jacob and I lie down to rest for the remainder of the night.

CHAPTER 21

I WAKE UP WITH what seems like an hour or two of sleep. What was once a busy and bustling headquarters is now completely empty. How does this happen? Not a word from anybody. I decide to pull my phone out of my pocket and try calling Bob again. It goes right away to "This phone number has been disconnected or is no longer in service," and I start thinking the worst.

Wait! Of course, why don't I call the phone number attached to the app that I created? I smile and shake my head. Why didn't I think of that first? So I call the number in the app, and right away, I hear a voice. After the initial spiel, I ask to speak with Bob. Within just a few moments, Bob gets on the phone. He says, "Good morning. This is Bob. How can I help you?"

I can't speak fast enough. I reply, "Bob! You guys are okay?"

I can hear the excitement in Bob's voice. "John! Where are you? Are you at our old location?"

I respond, "I am, but it's completely ransacked!"

Bob replies, "Don't worry, I'll send a guy to show you where we are now and explain everything when you get here."

"Thank you, Father, for keeping them safe," I pray. I look down at Jacob, and he's still snoozing. "Hey, buddy, it's time to wake up. Everybody is okay, and they are sending somebody to show us where the new headquarters is," I whisper to Jacob. Jacob sits up in bed and rubs his eyes. I pull him up, and we begin making our way back outside.

"John? Are you John Burton?" says this guy from the other side of the alley.

I reply, "Yes, I am John. Did Bob send you?"

He replies, "Yes, Bob sent me to show you the way to our new location. My name is Tony. It's truly an honor to meet you, sir."

I furl my eyebrows while being confused as to what in the world he is talking about. I ask, "What do you mean? It's an honor?"

He excitedly replies, "Everybody knows who you are, Mr. Burton! What you have created has done some amazing things for so many people, and I'm just thrilled to get to meet you!"

This is all so confusing. I leave the headquarters, and I only know a handful of people, and now all of a sudden, everybody knows who I am. I turn to Tony and say, "Well, I appreciate it. You might have me mixed up with somebody else. Bob will explain to you who I am when we get back."

Tony smiles and responds, "I don't think so, sir, but we aren't far." He is right, we aren't far from the new place. I think I can see it right up ahead.

Wow! This place is amazing. It's not slummy; it's actually quite nice. I walk through the front doors, and two receptionists stand and say, "Welcome, Mr. Burton." I nod and smile. They hit the buzzer to allow us through the double doors, and as the doors open up, I see this massive room. It's easily bigger than the original headquarters by triple. I start walking in, and everybody stops what they're doing and looks at me. Some of them stay seated, and others stand. They just stare at me, and I feel this very uneasy feeling in my stomach. Why are they all staring at me?

Up ahead, I can see Bob standing on a platform, and he looks at me and smiles. I am about halfway down the row, and Bob speaks into the microphone. "Allow me to introduce our founder, Mr. Burton!" Just then, everybody stands and starts clapping and cheering. I look down at Jacob, and he's just as shocked as I am. I get up to the front, and Bob grabs my hand and says, "Welcome home, brother! Maybe you could say a few words for our family." I stand there and realize this is Ma tovu ohalecha. This is what I created.

I step up to the microphone, and I'm still in shock, but then I just begin to speak. "Hi. I'm so surprised and flattered at the level of welcome my son and I received today. I don't know that I did anything to deserve the welcome that I got, but I'm thankful for it nonetheless. I'm so happy and excited that Ma tovu ohalecha has taken off the way it did. I'm also so thankful that you all share the vision that I had when I sat tirelessly and created the app that we are using today. For those of you that don't know, Ma tovu ohalecha is Hebrew for 'How fair are your tents.' This was chosen because Balaam in the book of Numbers 24:5 had the order to curse the Israelites but chose to bless them instead. We could sit by and curse our lives and make excuses for why we can't do this or why we can't do that. Rather, you get up every day and fight the good fight! I couldn't sit by and watch the government take our freedom and keep us from fulfilling that which we feel the need to do . . . to connect. Every person that is signed up and every group that is listed gets us another step closer to looking the government in the face and shouting, 'We won't sit by silently and allow YOU to take our freedoms. We serve a God on a higher seat, and His law supersedes yours! We won't go down without a fight, and as long as there is life in this body, we WILL FIGHT!'"

Everybody cheers and claps. Some of them are laughing and cheering, and others are cheering and crying. I can imagine that there are some who have lost as much as me or maybe more. This is an emotional thing for all of us. I turn and look at Jacob, and as everybody stands and cheers, he stands there, and I see a smile on his face and tears streaming down his cheeks. I get down on my knee, and I say to him, "Are you okay, buddy?"

He wipes the tears from his eyes and says, "I'm so proud that you are the man that God called you to be. I'm so proud of my dad and what you have done. I'm so glad you're my dad." I embrace my boy and cry. I feel like we have lost so much, and for my son to say he's proud of me, that means the world to me.

Bob walks up to the microphone and says, "Thanks, everybody. Let's do what we can do to get this to the world." Everybody begins to go about their daily activities, and Bob puts his hand on my shoulder. I stand, and he says, "Let's go sit over here and talk for a bit."

We sit, and Bob says, "I'm sure you have some questions, but let me tell you what happened, and that might clear up some questions. First, we were in the old headquarters, and we received word from one of our people, which are higher up the chain in the city, that the military knew about our headquarters, and we were a couple days away from a full military invasion. So we appealed to our people on the app by sending out a mass message and were asking for help by way of finances. We asked for money not only to move the headquarters, but we wanted to continue to upgrade the infrastructure to accommodate the users we have. We ended up getting pledges to help with a group tithe from all those people on a regular basis. As of right now, we are bringing in about $1 million a week in tithes from our groups, and the number grows every week.

"So we bought this place. Not only is the money helping us grow the infrastructure, but we're also using the money to feed the hungry here in Philly. Needless to say, the money is being put to great use. I would have called and let you know, but in the process of getting out of the old headquarters, I dropped my phone in some water and lost all my numbers. I tried getting my old number back so you could have called me, but they were having some trouble connecting the two accounts. Either way, I couldn't get in touch with you. We have VOIP now, which is much more efficient and is helping us to keep up with the demand.

"We are also making some contributions to the city to throw them off our trail and keep them out of our business. We have a nice place here, and we need to ensure that this work continues for a long time. I'm sorry I haven't included you more in the decisions, but many of these decisions needed to be made quickly. So what questions do you have for me?"

I start talking. "Listen, Bob, I left you in charge of this because I knew you were the person for the job. You don't answer to me. You answer to God. So thank you for keeping this ministry safe and doing a great job of keeping it moving forward. I also want to thank you for building me up so much to these people, but it really wasn't necessary. I didn't do this for recognition. I did it because people need other people."

Bob responds, "Look, I know why you did it, but I wanted everybody to know who was responsible for heeding the calling that God had on their life, and that was you!"

I look at Bob and smile. "Thanks, Bob. I appreciate that. This is an amazing place, and I couldn't have left it in better hands." We get up, and Bob starts showing us around the facility. As I start looking around, I realize something very drastic. "Where is Mary?"

Bob looks down and immediately feels sadness for me. "I'm sorry, John. She was captured just yesterday. Her and a couple other ladies were going around the area and talking to others about Jesus, and the one person Mary chose was an undercover agent. I would have told you, but I had no way of getting in touch with you. She is set to go on trial first thing tomorrow morning."

I look at Bob and say, "You know what, I may not be able to get her out of there, but I've seen too many miracles not to try!" I grab Jacob, and out the door, we go to see Mary.

CHAPTER 22

W E MAKE IT to town center, and even getting this far is challenging. We have to avoid all the officers and military to even get this far. However, by the grace of God, we manage to make it.

We get to the courthouse, and they check Jacob and me for metal objects and send us through the metal detector. We obviously have nothing on us, so I'm not too worried about that, although I'm very nervous that there are so many people here who can put an end to my life in a hurry. The only thing that keeps me motivated and moving forward is finding Mary.

This all seems so surreal. I feel like I was just here a few days ago, when I listened to my wife being sentenced to death. The smell is the same, and to most people, I think the smell is pretty typical for a courthouse. To me, however, this is the smell of death. This is where people go to die, and outside God, there is no hope of making it out of here alive when you're led in bound with handcuffs.

Jacob and I finally make it up to the courtroom, and we just find a seat fairly close to the front so that Mary will be able to see us. I'm still hopeful that we will get the opportunity to say something to her, anything. I would love to tell her that I love her, and she is worth coming here to see her. In the back of my mind, I can't help but feel as though they can't execute her. She's an old lady. What harm or danger can she possibly cause?

The officials start shuffling in the room, and I start seeing the attorneys making their way into the room. I notice there is no attorney for the accused, but why would I be surprised about that? They took our freedom of religion. Why wouldn't they take our other freedoms as well?

Just then, the prisoners shuffle in to the courtroom. There are about twenty-five of them in a line that take up the entire front row of the courtroom. I wonder what all these people have done.

I look, and I see Mary walk into the room. She looks so small between the two men who are in front and behind her. She doesn't belong in that group, and it is so upsetting that they even have her in there.

Mary looks up and scans the room, and immediately, she and I connect eyes. I see her smile, and I can begin to see tears in her eyes. I can imagine how she is feeling because I've been there. It's so good to see her! She looks just the same on the outside but looking a little rough from sitting in jail for two days.

She sits and immediately turns around in her seat to look at me. I lean forward, and I whisper loudly, "I love you, Grandma!" As I finish what I'm saying, we both smile, and I know right away that she knows everything that I wanted her to know.

"All rise! The honorable judge Tomkins presiding!" the bailiff exclaimed. The judge walks in and sits in his chair. He looks like an angry man and has one goal today, and that's to end religion.

I watch person after person stand before the judge, and each one is in trouble for some sort of religious crime. I have seen a few people who have been sentenced to death that weren't even of the Christian faith. That just goes to show you none of us are safe when our freedom of religion is trampled. However, each one, without much deliberation, is sentenced to death by firing squad in the town square.

One by one, they get sentenced, and I dread the moment when Mary has to stand before the judge and what that will mean. I look at Jacob, and I tell him, "Listen, buddy, I know this is really sad, and I'm sad for the people who are being put to death. However, no matter what the outcome is, we can't say anything, or we will get in trouble, okay?" He looks up at me and nods in affirmation.

Just then, Mary is called to stand and give account for her case. The district attorney begins to speak. "Your honor, she is being charged with one count of spoken religion and one count of written religion by way of a small religious book she had on her person when she was arrested."

The judge nods and then looks at Mary and says, "Ma'am, did you hear the charges that are being brought against you?"

Mary says, "Yes."

The judge asks, "Do you have any questions about these charges?"

Mary says, "No."

The judge then asks, "Ma'am, how do you plead?"

Mary responds, "I plead not guilty, Your Honor."

The judge looks down at his paperwork and then looks up at Mary. "Ma'am, you have acknowledged the charges. How can you plead not guilty?"

Mary replies, "You asked me if I had any questions about those charges, and I didn't have any questions about those charges. That has nothing to do with whether or not I agree with those charges."

The judge glances at his paperwork again and then asks, "Ma'am, were you speaking to an undercover agent about your deity? Yes or no."

Mary replies, "Yes."

The judge then proceeds to ask "Did you have a religious book in your possession that is referred to as a Holy Bible?"

Mary again replies, "Yes."

The judge asks, "Then how can you plead not guilty?"

Mary responds, "I'm pleading not guilty because I'm not guilty of a crime. Just like my savior standing before Pontius Pilate for crimes He didn't commit, I stand before you innocent. The court that my savior stood in front of was just as much a mock court as this one is."

The judge gets red in the face and quite angry. "Ma'am, I wouldn't advise you to address this court in such a tone. One more word against this court and I will hold you in contempt."

Mary quietly and calmly asks, "Judge, what will contempt do to me? Will it prolong the execution to keep me in jail for a couple more days? Will it fine me after I'm dead? Do with me as you will because you have no power over me that hasn't been given to you by my God!"

The judge pounds his gavel against his bench and yells, "Ma'am, you are now in contempt of this court!"

Mary smiles and tells the judge, "That's okay, Judge. I'm okay with that. One more thing and then I'll take whatever sentencing you choose to give me. I hope you find Jesus and His love and mercy before God's wrath finds you. It's not too late for you."

The judge snarls and looks at Mary with a disgusted look on his face. He then proceeds to cast his sentencing. "Ma'am, it is this court's decision to fine you $1,000 for your one count of spoken religion. It is this court's decision to fine you $1,000 for your one count of written religion." By this time, everybody is confused and dumbfounded. What in the world is going on, and what is the judge doing?

The judge then looks at Mary and smiles and then finishes up, "It is this court's decision, for one count of contempt, to sentence you to death by firing squad." He is just being nasty and giving her hope where there was none. What a despicable human being!

Mary smiles and then tells the judge, "Thank you, Judge, and God bless you!"

The judge's smile quickly vanishes, and then he yells at the bailiff, "Get her outta here!"

Mary then turns and looks at me and Jacob and smiles and then winks at us. I begin to cry, and she shakes her head no as if to tell me not to cry for her. Just then, Jacob stands and yells out, "Judge! You can't do that! She is a good woman! God will punish you for what you have done!" I look at Jacob, and I sigh and shake my head. He's his dad's son, all right.

The judge looks at Jacob and me and then commands the other bailiffs in the room to arrest us for the outburst. The judge has Jacob and me taken to the back room, and the judge walks in after a short while. "So I'm to assume you're one of those Christians as well. Is that correct?" Neither one of us respond. "Why don't you give me your names, and we'll go from there?" the judge asks. Again, neither one of us respond. The judge smiles. "That's okay. You don't have to speak. That just makes my job easier. We have a courtroom full of witnesses. That's all I need. Bailiff, take them to a holding cell."

Jacob and I are taken to a jail cell, where I guess we are going to wait for trial. I begin to pray. "Father, I think this was probably a bad idea. I'm sure we all have bad ideas from time to time. I just needed to see Mary one last time before I never get to see her again. Now I have endangered my life and my son's life. What am I to do? I don't know if I'm allowed to ask, but maybe You could perform another miracle like You did for me at the other police station that I was in. I would be so grateful! If that's not a possibility, perhaps You could at least get my son out of here, and I'll take the punishment. Father, we'll accept Your will and pray that it will be done. Amen."

Jacob and I sit in the jail cell with no knowledge of what's to come and what the outcome will be. I suppose that isn't unlike other times that we have encountered since all this unfolded. Since the beginning, we have been blinded as to what is going to happen.

Jacob looks up at me and says, "Dad, I heard you praying, and you said you wanted to see Mary again before you never get to see her again. Won't you get to see her in heaven?"

I look down at Jacob and smile. "You're right, son, we'll both get to see her in heaven."

Just then, I hear, "Ready, aim, FIRE!" I hear this four times, and undoubtedly, my sweet Mary was one of those who lost her life. I pray, "Father, tell her how much we love her and truly look forward to seeing her again. I don't imagine You will do that, but it never hurts to ask." Goodbye, Mary.

CHAPTER 23

I LIE IN MY bed just staring at the ceiling. I'm not entirely sure what time it is, maybe 2:00 a.m. Jacob is sleeping soundly, but I can't sleep. I begin to scan the room, just looking for something to occupy my mind. I notice some writing on the wall. I try to focus on the writing a bit so I can read it, and it's really hard to see with these eyes. I quietly get up out of bed and approach the writing. I see a bunch of initials and dates of former inmates. I then notice something familiar, something I haven't seen in a while. I see some familiar writing on the wall. It says, "If you find this, I love you so much, John, and my two babies, Jessica and Jacob. I'll see you soon. With all my love!" I can feel the tears welling up in my eyes as I realize this is the same cell that my beautiful wife was in before she was killed. I touch the wall where she wrote these words and just cry. I so desperately wish I could hold her one more time. I so desperately miss her hand on my face and the feel of her lips against mine. I miss looking into her beautiful blue eyes and her beautiful smiling face and seeing the worries and anxieties just melt away. She was one of the best things that ever happened to me.

I begin to pray. "Father, I miss my wife and Jessica so much. Losing somebody you love is so incredibly difficult. I'm just tired, Father. I'm tired in my heart, and I'm tired in my soul. I know we weren't promised any kind of life, but I'm praying that whatever outcome we have, You don't allow my boy to suffer. Please keep it quick for him, Father. I'll take the pain and suffering of death. I'm not above Your son, Jesus Christ, and I know He suffered as well. Please give me the wisdom to say and do the righteous things in the next few days so that everything I do brings glory to You. I love You, Father, and maybe I'll be seeing You soon."

I lie back down in bed, and I reflect on a day when Layna and I took the kids to boating. We had such an amazing day. We would do the tubing thing, boogie boarding, and skiing behind the boat. We laughed all day as each of us would wipe out. Looking back makes me smile. What an amazing day.

I drift off to sleep. I am standing across this great chasm, and I can see Layna holding a baby and Jessica standing next to her. I yell across, "I LOVE YOU!" They can't hear me though. It is so beautiful on the side that they're standing on. I can see them waving at me, but we can't speak to one another. I then see what appears to be a man walking up behind them. He is so bright that I can't make out his face. I can see him put his hands on Layna's and Jessica's shoulders. Wow, how incredible! That must be Jesus Christ. It has to be.

Suddenly, I feel something evil and ominous standing behind me. I turn and look, and I notice the skies are dark and smoky. There is fire everywhere and things on fire. I notice large animals appearing from the shadows of the ground. They have the bodies of a horse. I notice they have crowns on gold on their heads, but their faces are like a man's face. They have long hair like that of a woman and sharp teeth like a lion. They have these amazing breastplates and huge wings that make the ground shake when they move. They have tails like scorpions, and they look very scary. They appear to have one purpose, and that is to torment mankind. All of a sudden, they start chasing man and hurting them. They clearly have the power and size to kill them, but they will only hurt them to cause pain.

I cry out, "Father! Help us!" After I cry out, I see one of the beasts look over at me and start running toward me. I begin running away, but I am no match for the speed of this beast. I can feel his power approaching from behind me, and I look over my shoulder, and before he grabs me with his powerful jaws, I wake up.

I sit up in my bed, and I am sweating profusely. That was a horrible dream! What in the world was that all about? Why would God give me a dream like that?

I lie in bed, just pondering the dream. I hear God tell me, "These things are coming. Do what you can!" That's it? That's all? Do what I can? I can't do anything! I'm stuck in a jail cell. It is then I start realizing God doesn't care about my location. I quickly apologize to God and start coming up with a game plan.

"Hey, guard! Guard!" I say loudly to get their attention.

I see the guard approach, and he asks, "What do you want?"

I ask, "Would you mind if I were to get a pen and paper so I could write some things?"

Without saying anything, he quickly goes and grabs a couple of sheets of paper and a pen to give to me. "Here you go," says the guard.

I say, "Hey, wait, let me ask you a question." The guard stops and looks at me. I ask, "Do you know what they're doing to us and for what reason?"

He looks at me and says, "Yeah, I know why."

I ask him, "How do you feel about that?"

The guard responds, "I'm not paid to feel a certain way. I'm paid to keep you here until they decide what they want to do to you."

I smile at him and say, "Come on, that's a cop-out. You're a human being with human feelings, and your opinion matters. How do you feel about that?"

He puts his head down and says, "I don't like it, but what can I do about it?"

I reply, "You can have compassion. You can still express love, right?" He nods yes. I ask him, "You were going to church before all of this went down, right?"

The guard replies, "Yeah I was. I hadn't been going very long, but I didn't want to put my family in jeopardy. I'm sure God understands."

I respond to his statement, "So let me ask you a question. If one of your kids were to disown you because they felt like it was the right thing to do, would you be okay with that?"

"How could disowning me be the right thing to do?" the guard asks.

I respond, "I'm just asking. They feel like it's the right thing to do for them. Would you be okay with that?"

He shakes his head and says, "No, that's wrong. You don't just disown somebody. You are family, and you stick with them! Right or wrong, good or bad, they are your family."

I smile at him and ask, "Is God your family?"

He quickly rebuttals, "Wait, that's not the same thing!"

I quickly respond, "Isn't it? God calls you His son. He sends His only heavenly son to Earth to die on a cross for your sins. He does this so you don't have to worry about hell, but you have a way to God and heaven that nobody ever had before Jesus. That is the greatest expression of love I have ever seen, and you're taking that love and saying you don't want it because you're afraid for you and your family. I couldn't do that to my heavenly Father."

The guard begins to cry. "I never looked at it like that. I can't believe I did that to Him."

As I have tears rolling down my cheeks, I reply, "Here's the good news, my brother. God sent His son to die for us so all we need to do is ask for forgiveness and turn away from that which displeases the Father. Look at Peter. He loved Jesus Christ very much but still denied Him three times. Look at King David, a man after God's own heart and did this horrible thing with Bathsheba and Uriah. It's not the act that we need to focus on. It's the act of getting up, dusting yourself off, and getting back into fellowship with God that matters the most. What do you say?"

The guard looks up at me and smiles and says, "You're right! I will never turn my back on God again, no matter what that costs me."

I smile and shake his hand. "It's going to get bad, brother, and very difficult, but the reward in the end is far better than anything you can imagine. Just hold yourself and your family close to the cross, and don't stop until you get to heaven!"

I give him directions on where he can find Bob because I'm confident Bob will take care of him. I tell the guard, "Hey, just tell him that John Burton sends you, and he will take good care of you."

The guard responds, "I sure will! Thanks for caring enough for me to talk to me."

I smile and reply, "You got it, brother. Now let me get this letter written so you can give it to Bob for me."

I carefully outline all the details of the dream on the paper that the guard gave me. As I am writing it all down, the Holy Spirit starts giving me insight as to what this dream means. This is the end; that's what this dream is. This is the tribulation that the Bible speaks about. I think it's getting very close, and God wants me to let Bob know.

I ask Bob in the letter to send this out to everybody through the app so they will know that the end is very near. We absolutely need to be very ready. I begin praying, "Father, You're so amazing! I'm still astounded how You know what we need and when we need it. I pray in Your name that this letter finds Bob in good health and that those who read its message will prepare themselves for that which is coming. I love You, Father!"

"Hey, guard." I speak. He walks back over to my cell. "I'm sorry, what's your name? I never asked," I ask the guard.

He smiles and says, "My name is Dan."

I look at him and grab his hand and then put my other hand over both our hands. "Dan, it was truly my pleasure to get to talk to you. No matter what happens, I truly look forward to seeing you in the hereafter. God bless you, my brother."

I hand him the letter, and he puts it into his pocket and quickly whisks out the door. This is all almost over.

CHAPTER 24

I PRAY THAT DAN finds his way to Bob. I really feel as though this dream is paramount for those who are here. It is a revelation to those who have been praying for divine intervention. It is a way for God to let us know that this thing is just about over and that Jesus will be coming to collect us very soon.

I lie back down on my bed and glance over at the wall where my beautiful Layna wrote her final words to us. I don't think she would have imagined what would have transpired for us to be here and that we would have lost Jessica to a terrible illness. I truly look forward to seeing her and embracing her again, but I'm not looking forward to how I'm getting there. I've never been shot and don't know how painful it will be.

About that time, one of the other guards walks up to my cell and says, "Burton! Time to go. The judge wants to see you." I get up and wake Jacob up. He puts cuffs on our wrists and our ankles. I guess they're afraid we're going to try and run.

We start making our way downstairs where the courtroom is. I can see people lined up in the halls. Some of them are reporters, and some are just people watching. I tell Jacob, "It's okay, buddy. Just smile and don't let them think we're bothered by this." He musters up what courage and strength he has and smiles and keeps walking.

We walk into the courtroom, much in the same way that Mary did when she was shuffled in. The room is full of people, and many of them are very quiet and somber as we walk in. As I sit next to all the other inmates, I feel the butterflies in my stomach. I'm very nervous and anxious for what is about to come.

"All rise! The honorable judge Tomkins presiding!" the bailiff exclaimed. The judge walks in again, and truthfully, nothing has changed about this man. He still looks angry and looks like he hates the world. I expect that today will end much like it did the day that Mary was present in the courtroom and awaiting sentencing.

The judge begins calling case after case up front, and every single one of them ends the same way. They all end with death by firing squad. Jacob looks up at me while sitting next to me, and I can see the panic on his face. I look down at him and smile. "Listen, buddy, we knew this was going to happen. Be strong, and we will be with Mom and Jessica soon." He smiles and nods yes. I'm so proud of him. To be that young and facing death is something that I can't comprehend.

It happens in slow motion. I hear the words "The people of the state versus John and Jacob Burton." I stand, and Jacob stands, and we shuffle to the front of the courtroom, where we're instructed to sit. The judge looks at us and says, "Well, if it isn't our outspoken ones. I trust you will be able to contain yourselves today. Am I correct?"

I look up at the judge and say, "Yes, Your Honor, we will do our best to contain ourselves."

The judge shakes his head and says, "You are being charged with two counts of religious speech and two counts of contempt of this court. Do you understand these charges."

I reply, "I understand the charges, but I don't understand how we're being charged with two counts of religious speech."

The judge responds, "Your child said, and I quote 'God will punish you for what you have done.' Did your son say these words?"

I reply, "Yes, he did, but how is that two counts of religious speech?"

The judge smirks and says, "Because he is a minor. That makes you responsible for what he said. So you'll both be punished for that. With that being said, how do you plead?"

I look at him and say, "Does it matter how I plead? You're just going to do what you want to do anyway, right?"

The judge pounds his gavel against his bench and says, "Don't you get mouthy with me in my courtroom, or I will hold you in contempt again!"

I reply, "Your Honor, do you honestly believe you're going to shut the mouths of all Americans when it comes to their religious views? You can shoot all the people that you want, but the fact remains there are always going to be people willing to live for God and even die for God. However, something you're not thinking about is this, if you remove this freedom of religion from our country, all you're successfully doing is removing the core of how this country was founded and what made this country the greatest country on the face of the planet. If you remove the ability for people to have a faith in their deity, you are living in a country where people will stop having a conscience, and crime will become a bigger problem than you have ever seen. My God is a moral compass for a lot of people, the same people who might end up doing bad things otherwise. However, to answer your question, I plead not guilty."

The judge smiles at me and says, "I didn't figure you would be able to contain yourself. Your little rant won't change anything." As the judge utters those words, he starts seeing the face of those around the courtroom. He begins to see the faces of anger and determination on those faces in the courtroom. He looks back over at John and says, "Mr. Burton, the decision to remove freedom of religion was done for various reasons, and our elected officials found this important. I'm required to uphold the law, which was laid. I'm acknowledging your plea of not guilty, and I'm saying that you are guilty. I'm going to have to make an example of you and your dangerous thinking so that if others share in your dangerous views, they will think differently in the future."

The judge looks down at me and Jacob and says, "Please stand for your sentencing. Jacob Burton, you are found guilty of crimes of the state and are to be sentenced to death by firing squad. John Burton, because of your views and the dangers of those views, I'm ordering a flogging in the town square. After your flogging, you are going to be crucified like your deity until you are dead. Bailiffs, take them away."

Well, that is definitely not what I was expecting. I figured I was going to suffer a little bit, but that is more than I expected. I don't regret saying what I said. I feel like there are some in that courtroom who understand what I was saying, and they are going to bite the bullet and do the right thing by God.

We wait in the hallway for the rest of the inmates to get their sentencing. Jacob looks up at me in worry. I look down at him and say, "Hey, it's okay. We're going home. Don't worry about me. You're not going to suffer. It's going to be over before you even realize it. Be strong, buddy! I love you so much!"

Everybody has received their sentencing, and we are all being shuffled outside. I can see everybody who was in the courthouse is making their way outside to witness all that is going to take place. I wonder what people's infatuation with death is. To watch people die is so disturbing to me.

We finally get outside, and I see where they are going to crucify me, but it isn't a cross; it's just a straight pole. I don't think I have ever seen anything like that. I thought they were all crosses, not sure how that's going to work.

Everybody is put into position in front of the firing squad, but they are given strict orders that nobody will die until I am hanging on the pole. They bring me over to a wooden structure and bind my hands to the wooden beam. They cut my shirt and pants off. I look back, and I can see the guy holding the whip, and he rears back to make his first strike.

CHAPTER 25

THE FIRST STRIKE hits me, and it feels like nothing I have ever felt before. It stings and burns like having an open sore and pouring alcohol on it. It also feels like it's splitting my skin open. I guess it could be. I can't really tell.

My mind instantly goes to a movie that I saw where Jesus was being whipped. I know what He was feeling had to be worse because His whip was designed to pull flesh off, but mine is just a normal whip with what appears to be leather straps. Through the pain, I manage to feel a sense of pride to know that I am suffering for the namesake of Christ. I suppose it's very similar to the crucifixion of Peter when he was hung upside down. I'm honored to being killed like my savior.

The straps hit me for the second time. This time really hurts worse than the first time. I'm not sure what makes this instance hurt worse, but it is at least five times worse than the first. The third strike hits my back, and it hurts but doesn't hurt as bad as the first two. The fourth, fifth, and sixth strikes hit, and I can feel it, but it's getting to the point of not hurting anymore. I assume my body is shutting down feeling back there, or maybe my body's natural anesthetic is kicking in.

I can hear people in the crowd gasping as I am being flogged. I sense that nobody is expecting this. I even get the impression that it is more than they have bargained for, although I can't imagine people being so twisted as to want to watch public shootings and floggings.

As I am standing there strapped to the pole, the judge walks up behind me and says, "So how are you feeling about your God now?"

I respond, "I'm feeling so much closer to Him now. Thank you so much for allowing me to experience a small piece of what my savior went through."

In a fit of rage, the judge orders that I be turned around and whipped from the front. So the guy holding the whip turns me around so that my belly and chest will get whipped now. I don't think I'm a glutton for punishment, but I can't let them think they are winning. My savior ultimately won, and He doesn't lose!

The guy pulls his arm up for his first strike and down comes the whip. Oh my goodness, the pain is worse in the front than it was in the back. Why did I have to open my mouth? Maybe I should have just kept silent and let him do what he was going to do. I know Jesus kept silent during a part of the time in front of Pontius Pilate. I suppose it's too late now.

I open my eyes and watch as the whip keeps coming down and striking me. I look out into the crowd, and I am shocked to see so many faces I know. The first person I see is Bob. He is crying, and he has his hands folded together as if he is praying for me. I see Dan to my right. He is trying to not cry, so I smile at him in hopes to help him overcome his sadness. Then I see somebody whom I didn't expect to see; it's somebody whom I hadn't seen in a while. I see Tony standing there. Tony is the truck driver whom I spent all that time with getting back to Philadelphia. He has a very distraught look on his face and is clearly very upset.

I look back over at Bob, and he pulls the letter out of his pocket and nods yes. I know now that Bob got the letter that I sent with Dan to deliver to him. I'm so proud that Dan is going to be going to heaven with me someday. I made a difference in his life and set his family up with people who will encourage his faith and point him in the right direction.

I glance over at Jacob, and I can see him crying. My poor son; I hate that he has to live in such times as these. He didn't get much of a life or a chance of one, and that breaks my heart. In some ways, I feel like a failure as a father because I couldn't protect my kids. I couldn't keep them from harm. It's my duty as a father to protect them and keep them safe. Then on the other side, I feel like I did exactly what I was supposed to do. I set them up for success in heaven, and they know a loving heavenly Father because of Layna and me.

I begin to pray. "Father, I thank You for being here with me today. Even now, I believe the pain that I feel is real, but I also believe You are protecting me from some of the pain and shielding me from it. I pray, Father, that You ease the heart of those watching that love me and help them to understand that I'm soon going home. For those who are watching and anxiously anticipating my death, I pray for their heart, Father. I pray that the Holy Spirit finds a way to minister to them and come to a realization of who You are before it's too late. I pray that what I started with the app and the ability for others to get to find others to worship with continues and gets stronger. I love You, Father, and I'll see You soon."

After several strikes on the front side, we are finally done. The judge snidely walks back up to me and says, "How are you feeling about God now?"

I turn my head and smile at him and say, "I love my God so much, and with what little time I have left, I'm going to be praying the love of Jesus Christ over you."

The judge's lips begin to quiver, and he immediately says, "Enough of this! Send him over there to be executed by firing squad!"

I have to admit, I can't say that I'm disappointed that he chose not to crucify me. I wasn't really looking forward to that. At least my pain and suffering is nearly over now.

Some of the guards escort me over to the row of inmates who are about to be executed by firing squad. As I make my way over there, I pray again, "Father, as promised, I pray that You touch the heart of the judge. I sense that he got a glimpse of the love of God. I pray that he continues to seek Your face and that he comes to a realization that he needs You in his life. Thank You, Father, for hearing my prayer."

I get put into place next to Jacob. I look down at him, and I say, "Be strong, my son, it's almost over." He pushes his little hand up into mine and then smiles up at me. I'm so proud of him and how brave he is.

The judge gets up in front of the crowd and says, "Listen up! Anybody who shares the same beliefs and obstinance will meet the same end as John Burton here. God is fake, and it was all made up a long time ago to control people!"

I then yell out, "Isn't that what the government is doing to us? Aren't they controlling us? The difference is, we're standing here in front of the firing squad, and the government is not! You say that God isn't real, but there have been hundreds of people, maybe thousands of people, who have died in this very spot because they wouldn't renounce the name of Jesus Christ. Does that sound like people who have lost their minds? I believe it's the contrary. I believe if people are willing to die for this, there must be a lot of truth in it. I pray you find that truth before you meet a horrible end. I also believe if things keep going the way they're going, you're going to see something this country has never seen and death it has never experienced. Mark my words, those who are still here will not stand idly by and do nothing. Even now, they are working and making sure that the great news of Jesus Christ continues!"

The judge yells out, "That's enough of this hogwash! Firing squad! Take aim and fire on three!"

Jacob squeezes my hand and tightly shuts his eyes, and I squeeze his hand back and say, "Father, help us!"

"Three . . . Two . . . One . . . Fire!"

CHAPTER 26

I LOOK DOWN AFTER hearing the shot, and I don't see anything. Did they miss? I look down at Jacob, and he looks fine too. I'm a bit confused. What happened?

The firing squad is putting their guns away and walking away, and the judge is walking back inside. I don't understand what's going on. Are they letting us go? Then it dawns on me; they didn't miss. I look down at the ground, and there, Jacob and I lie on the ground. I look down at Jacob and ask him, "Are you okay?"

He smiles and looks up at me. "I'm okay! That didn't hurt at all!"

Just then, Jacob and I start ascending. Oh my! Is this heaven that I'm heading toward? I hope so! Jacob and I are ascending hand in hand. We finally get to a place that is so beautiful, and there is a path there.

We begin walking down this path, and the smell in the air is the most beautiful and fragrant smell I have ever smelled. I look at the trees that I see along the path, and they are perfect in every way. I see maple trees, pines, hickory trees, but they are perfect. There are no leaves on the ground and no needles on the ground because nothing here dies. I see flowers on the ground that I have never seen before. Their beauty is unparalleled from any other flower I have ever even read about.

As we walk a bit further, I see this creek that is probably twenty to thirty feet across. I can't tell how deep it is because the water is crystal clear. I can't tell how fast the water is even moving because there is no white water, and it is so pure. I invite Jacob to take a drink with me. "Hey, let's take a sip." We kneel, and I cup my hand to get some water in it. I bring the water up to my lips, and I cannot believe how wonderful it tastes. I have never tasted water so clean and pure in all my life. I look down at Jacob and say, "Come on, buddy, I have a feeling the best is yet to come!"

We walk over the bridge, and as we continue down the path, things just keep getting brighter and more beautiful. I can see what appears to be a city up ahead. As we get through the trees and get into the clearing, I can see exactly what it is. It's a beautiful and amazing city. Words cannot even describe the beauty and magnificence that I'm seeing. As I gaze upon the city, I begin to cry. The awe of the city is overwhelming. Never have I seen anything more beautiful. The walls were a rainbow of colors. As I get closer, I can see that there are jewels that are making the walls colorful. It is essentially a rainbow of brilliance.

I see that the gates are immaculate and beautiful. They appear to be some sort of white and glimmering substance. Then I realize, I remember the Bible speaking of pearls or pearl gates. Wow! That is just so breathtaking and beautiful.

I sit on a boulder and just try and soak it all in, and I can't get enough. I can see why people who have been here didn't want to leave. It's pure paradise, and there is no other way of describing it.

While Jacob and I sit there, I can see one of the gates opening up. I can see some figures of some people standing there. I look down at Jacob and say, "Well, buddy, I guess we better get in there."

We jump and start making our way to the city. As we get closer, I can see that it's my beautiful wife and my two amazing children standing there waiting for us. I begin to cry as I realize that this isn't a dream. I have so desperately longed to hold them again, and this time it will be forever. As I stand there crying, I see another figure coming up from behind and puts his hands on the shoulders of Jessica and Layna. I then realize that it's Jesus Christ. I then fall on my face and begin to cry. I'm overwhelmed with joy and awe that I cannot contain it.

As I lie there crying, somebody kneels in front of me and pulls my face up. As I look up, I can see that it's my savior, the Man whom I have lived for so many years and whom I ultimately died for. He smiles at me and then uses His thumb to wipe the tears off my face. He then pulls me up and says to me, "Well done, my good and faithful servant. Enter into your rest."

I see Layna standing there crying, and Jacob has already made his way in there. I begin crying again and feel myself being pulled to them uncontrollably. In a moment, I embrace my beautiful wife. We cry together because we are so happy to be in each other's arms again. I feel like it's been so long. I put her face between my hands and tell her, "I have missed you something awful! It is such a joy to see you again, and we will never have to part company again."

I look over at Jessica, and I can feel the tears running down my cheeks. "I love you so much, my beautiful daughter. I was so heartbroken when I couldn't help you on Earth. I'm glad you're here though."

She looks at me and says, "Daddy, thank you for teaching me the right way. Thank you for showing me the love of Jesus Christ. I'm here because of you and Mom." I smile at her and touch her face.

I then look at the other little girl whom my wife has been holding in my dreams. I say, "You must be my other beautiful girl. I'm sorry we never got a chance to meet on Earth, but I'm glad we will get to spend forever together."

She smiles and says, "Me too! I can't wait!"

I turn around and gaze into heaven and put my arms around my family. Layna then looks at me and says, "I have so much to show you. There is this lady that I want you to meet who I'm fascinated with. Her name is Mary. She said she was from Philadelphia too."

I smile and say, "I can't wait."

We begin our journey in heaven, and we live eternally happily ever after.